Praise for the Sudoku Mysteries

Ghost Sudoku

"These are fast, fun reads with enough intrigue to satisfy any mystery reader, and the added bonus of included puzzles. If you're not up on your sudoku-solving skills, there are tips and clues to help you get started. If you're already a puzzle person, you'll enjoy the puzzles." —*CA Reviews*

Killer Sudoku

"Puzzles are included for fans of sudoku but, fans or not, readers will enjoy this fast-paced mystery." —*Cozy Library*

Sinister Sudoku

"A wonderful addition to Ms. Morgan's Sudoku Mystery series! The narrative hits the ground running, incorporating sudoku strategy with a treasure hunt and a tantalizing whodunit! I look forward to more!" —*The Romance Readers Connection*

Murder by Numbers

"Kaye Morgan has written a cleverly constructed mystery that reflects the finely crafted sudoku puzzles that are included for fans to enjoy." —*The Mystery Gazette*

"Whether you are interested in sudoku or not, this mystery is fun and challenging." —*MyShelf.com*

Death by Sudoku

"Kaye Morgan is a talented storyteller who will go far in the mystery genre." —*The Best Reviews*

"Puzzles and codes surround a vast pattern of murder." —*Spinoff Reviews*

Celebrity Sudoku

Kaye Morgan

BERKLEY PRIME CRIME, NEW YORK

THE BERKLEY PUBLISHING GROUP
Published by the Penguin Group
Penguin Group (USA) Inc.
375 Hudson Street, New York, New York 10014, USA
Penguin Group (Canada), 90 Eglinton Avenue East, Suite 700, Toronto, Ontario M4P 2Y3, Canada
(a division of Pearson Penguin Canada Inc.)
Penguin Books Ltd., 80 Strand, London WC2R 0RL, England
Penguin Group Ireland, 25 St. Stephen's Green, Dublin 2, Ireland (a division of Penguin Books Ltd.)
Penguin Group (Australia), 250 Camberwell Road, Camberwell, Victoria 3124, Australia
(a division of Pearson Australia Group Pty. Ltd.)
Penguin Books India Pvt. Ltd., 11 Community Centre, Panchsheel Park, New Delhi—110 017, India
Penguin Group (NZ), 67 Apollo Drive, Rosedale, North Shore 0632, New Zealand
(a division of Pearson New Zealand Ltd.)
Penguin Books (South Africa) (Pty.) Ltd., 24 Sturdee Avenue, Rosebank, Johannesburg 2196,
South Africa

Penguin Books Ltd., Registered Offices: 80 Strand, London WC2R 0RL, England

This is a work of fiction. Names, characters, places, and incidents either are the product of the author's imagination or are used fictitiously, and any resemblance to actual persons, living or dead, business establishments, events, or locales is entirely coincidental. The publisher does not have any control over and does not assume any responsibility for author or third-party websites or their content.

CELEBRITY SUDOKU

A Berkley Prime Crime Book / published by arrangement with Tekno Books

PRINTING HISTORY
Berkley Prime Crime mass-market edition / December 2010

Copyright © 2010 by Penguin Group (USA) Inc.
Sudoku puzzles and diagrams by Kaye Morgan.
Cover illustration by Trisha Krauss.
Interior text design by Laura K. Corless.

ISBN: 978-0-425-23827-1

BERKLEY® PRIME CRIME
Berkley Prime Crime Books are published by The Berkley Publishing Group,
a division of Penguin Group (USA) Inc.,
375 Hudson Street, New York, New York 10014.
BERKLEY® PRIME CRIME and the PRIME CRIME logo are trademarks of Penguin Group (USA) Inc.

PRINTED IN THE UNITED STATES OF AMERICA

10 9 8 7 6 5 4 3 2 1

In past books in this series, I've thanked various members of my family. This time around, I'd like to express my appreciation to the Berkley Prime Crime family for all they've done to make the Sudoku Mysteries a success . . . especially Michelle Vega, who aided, abetted, and edited.

Many thanks to you all.

1

"So, Rusty, what do you want?" Liza Kelly asked. The dog definitely wanted something—he had his best begging face on.

The Irish setter mix headed immediately for the kitchen door and tried to nose down the leash hanging from the doorknob.

"A walk, is it? Not so fast. I still have to finish my tea." Liza followed him into the kitchen, her cup in her hand, and took a sip.

The four glass panels set in the door gave a view of her piece of Maiden's Bay, Oregon—Hackleberry Avenue, to be exact, a pretty quiet street this time of the morning.

Maybe you should have gone with reinforced glass after the break-in. That annoying voice in the back of her head started up a long-running argument. *Or even solid wood. It might be safer, if you're going to keep getting involved in murders.*

"I don't get involved in murders," Liza muttered. "I write a column about sudoku that's syndicated all over the country, and I still do publicity work for Michelle Markson down in L.A."

Rusty looked up at her, his head cocked to one side. Then he launched into a series of barks and whines.

"You're right. I should move faster. And I'm talking to myself." Liza finished her tea and got the leash. She clicked it onto Rusty's collar and opened the door just in time for the postal delivery. No wonder Rusty was barking.

The letter carrier arrived at the mailbox, reached into his bag, and came out with a very large package. Liza could see it wouldn't fit, but the guy spent a couple of minutes trying to find the magic angle. Then he headed for the door, drawing a low growl from Rusty.

"Quiet, you," Liza told the dog. "He may be carrying a can of Mace." She closed the door on Rusty and headed down the path to meet the mailman.

"Sent Priority," he said. "I guess they really wanted you to get it." He passed the bulky package to Liza, added a few envelopes, and headed back to the sidewalk.

"Is that a present from an admirer?" a hopeful voice called from off to Liza's left. She turned to see her next-door neighbor, Elise Halvorsen, appear from behind the shrubbery. The older woman's gardening clothes were slightly muddy, but her eyes were bright with interest.

"No such luck, Mrs. H.," Liza replied. "It's business."

"Are you doing a sudoku book?" Mrs. Halvorsen asked, her eyes still on the package.

Liza heard a bark from behind and turned to see Rusty with his paws on one of the bottom windowpanes, peering out at her.

Looks as if everybody's curious, Liza thought, leading the way back to her kitchen. Rusty gave Mrs. H. a big welcome, barking and capering around. Smile lines filled the older woman's round face as she bent to pet him.

She quickly straightened as a weird noise came from her

pocket. "Text message," Mrs. Halvorsen explained, digging out a phone.

After squinting at the tiny screen, she sighed and began tapping on the keys. "And this is just to send an answer."

Mrs. H. brought her index finger down. "Ed—that's two taps on the number three for *E*, bip-bip, then pause for that to set in, and another hit on three for *D*, pause, hit zero for a space, three times on six for *O*, bip-bip-bip, two on the five for *K*, bip-bip, and then send."

She gave Liza a look of embarrassment mixed with exasperation. "I definitely have to upgrade to a phone with a keyboard. My finger is going to fall off with all this rigmarole."

"If you get a keyboard, you'll be complaining about your thumbs," Liza told her, then began to laugh. "And didn't you get this phone just a month ago? You're turning into that white-haired lady on the cell phone commercial with the BFF."

"Well, I am white-haired," Mrs. H. said.

"And instead of a BFF, you've got an Ed that you're saying 'okay' to. What's all that about?" Liza was fond of Mrs. H., but her neighbor was an inveterate matchmaker. Now Liza had the chance to turn the tables.

Mrs. Halvorsen's face got a little pinker. "He's a nice widower about two towns over who asked if I'd like to go to the movies. Since I didn't have the finger strength to ask if they had low-fat, low-sodium popcorn, I just said okay."

"Way to go, Mrs. H.!" Liza said as she removed the wrapping from her package to reveal a telephone-book-sized binder.

"Are you going back to school?" Mrs. H. asked.

"I'll have to study this a little," Liza admitted. "This is the production info for *D-Kodas*."

"Oh, the game show you're going to be on."

"For about two seconds," Liza said. "They decided they

wanted some celebrity puzzle experts to create the stuff the celebrity contestants have to decode."

She broke off, still feeling a little funny about that. Yes, she was well-known in the fairly obscure world of Sudoku Nation, but her celebrity status came more from finding a couple of murderers than from providing a daily puzzle fix.

"I'm sure you'll do just fine," Mrs. Halvorsen said loyally.

"Well, I sent the puzzles in, along with Will Singleton and Wanda Penny, who does acrostics." Liza shrugged. "They just want to tape us giving a couple of explanations and answering a few questions to use as filler between rounds of competition." She paused for a second. "I was going to ask if you could take care of Rusty while I was gone."

"He'll get lonely, left on his own here for a week." Translated, that was Mrs. H. warning she wouldn't be responsible for any damage Rusty might do.

"It won't be that long," Liza quickly said.

Mrs. Halvorsen gave her a puzzled look. "But the ads on TV talk about Celebrity *Week* on *D-Kodas*."

"It will only take a day to tape five shows," Liza explained, "and I agreed to come in a day early." She gave her neighbor a crooked smile. "That's the difference between us pseudo-celebrities and the real ones—the TV people feel free to impose on our schedules."

"Well, I'll certainly be glad to take care of Rusty." Mrs. H. stopped as Rusty responded to his name with a loud woof. "We'll have a good time, won't we, you large, silly dog?"

Rusty seemed to nod, lolling his tongue out of his mouth.

Mrs. Halvorsen watched with interest as Liza opened the binder. "So what do you have to study?"

"It's not so much studying as familiarizing myself," Liza said. "This section here covers the whole production crew for the show, lighting, cameramen, set and makeup people . . ." She paged through. "Here are the producers, the director, the cast . . ."

"I always liked that Wish Dudek," Mrs. H. said, pointing at a smiling publicity photo of the show's host.

"He is a nice guy," Liza said. "I must have told you he gave me a lift in his plane."

"Is he married these days?" Mrs. Halvorsen asked in a suspiciously indifferent tone.

Liza rolled her eyes. Her neighbor was ever ready, willing, and able to try and fix people up. "Definitely married, with a daughter in college." Liza stopped at another page. "Here are the celebrity guests."

"You call these stars?" Mrs. H. sniffed. "Most of them I wouldn't cross the street to see. "Claudio Day, I see him sometimes on the TV."

Liza nodded. "He's a football player. And Chard Switzer is in that sitcom . . ."

Mrs. H. made a face. "I don't watch that." She pointed at another publicity shot. "Forty Oz.—isn't he the one who shouts awful words in his songs?"

"He has a certain reputation," Liza admitted. "And they're not stars; they're celebrities."

"Well, I think Lolly Popovic is a star—she's been on shows since she was a kid," Mrs. H. argued. "And this latest one—*Newport Riche*—she's the only reason to watch."

"I'll be sure to tell her that," Liza said. "Would you like an autograph?"

"She'd be about the only one," Mrs. Halvorsen said. "Who is this Samantha Pang?"

Liza had to consult the book for the answer. "She's this year's winner for the Leland Prize in Mathematics. I wonder if that will give her any advantage with sudoku."

"She looks like a nice girl from her picture." Mrs. H. nodded approvingly, then frowned. "Not like that awful Ritz Tarleton."

"What?" Liza's gaze shot down the page to where a little dirt dribbled off Mrs. Halvorsen's gardening glove onto a picture of Ritz Tarleton. Apparently she'd changed from redhead to blond, but her portrait still showed her usual inch of grown-out roots—and the usual smug smile on her sharp, faintly foxy features.

What the hell is she doing on the show? The words nearly burst from her lips, but Liza clamped them shut. Even so, something of her response must have shown.

"I remember you had some trouble with that girl's father last winter." That was more than Mrs. H. usually said about the murder of her art thief brother and the wild search for a missing Mondrian.

"Ritz was one of the model prisoners in my sudoku class at Seacoast Correctional," Liza said a little grimly. Poor little rich girl Ritz hadn't impressed her with either her sudoku-solving ability or the predatory way Ritz went after Kevin Shepard, Liza's friend and maybe more.

She may be a B-list celebrity, but that put her on my S-list, Liza thought. *Ritz wasn't one of the people the production staff mentioned. How did she push herself onto* D-Kodas?

Liza was still puzzling over this unwelcome addition to the celebrity lineup three days later as she flew down to Los Angeles. The show's production people had been downright evasive, but she didn't want to ask her business partner, Michelle Markson, to get some answers. Availing herself of the power of Hollywood's female warlord of publicity would be like killing a fly with a sledgehammer.

Leaning back in her seat, Liza closed her eyes. Frankly, she was too tired to think about it anymore. After getting up before the sun rose, driving to Portland, and jumping through all the security hoops, she decided to devote the next two hours to sleeping.

The sound of the pilot's voice announcing their final approach woke Liza up. She blearily looked out the window to take in the smoggy vista of beautiful Los Angeles.

When the plane finally taxied to the Jetway, Liza got up and retrieved her carry-on bag. Too many journeys for the Markson Associates agency had taught Liza to keep her stuff nearby—and to travel light. This time the bag was fuller than usual for a two-day stay. But then, Liza had to mix and match outfits for the fictional "Celebrity Week" tomorrow's taping was supposed to cover.

Hooking the bag's strap over her shoulder, Liza deplaned and headed for the main concourse, looking for a driver with the usual little sign bearing her name.

Instead . . .

"Hey, Liza!" She turned to find Michael Langley waving at her through the crowd—her kinda-sorta-almost-ex-husband, if they ever got around to signing the divorce papers. A year ago, she'd have scribbled her name and been done with it. But as it came closer to reality, neither she nor Michael seemed particularly eager—or willing—to pick up the pen.

Michael made his way through the early-morning travelers and took Liza's bag. His unruly dark curls seemed even more tousled than usual, his heavy-lidded eyes about as red as Liza's felt.

"What are you doing here?" she asked. "You look as if you were up all night with your poker buddies."

He shook his head. "I've been working on an indie film that's shooting at Atotori Studios. You know, they rent out the facilities to whoever can pay—like the folks producing *D-Kodas*." Michael grinned. "And when they were discussing getting a car for you, I just happened to be around and volunteered my services." The grin faded a little. "What I didn't count on was a major rewrite session that lasted until about six o'clock."

Liza put out her hand. "In that case, I'm driving. Give me the keys."

Their first stop was the hotel where Liza was supposed to stay. It was actually an airport hotel, but Liza didn't much mind that, considering how close it was to the studio. After checking in and leaving her bag, they headed for the front gate of Atotori Studios. In the old days, the Mammoth Studios gate had been a landmark. It looked a little funny with the Japanese name on top.

Liza actually found herself at the end of a short line. As she waited, she heard a voice call out, "Yo! Betty!"

When she turned to look, Liza found herself staring into the business end of a video camera.

"What the—" she began as the cameraman scampered away from studio security. Liza turned to Michael. "What the hell was that?"

He only shrugged. "I forget you haven't been down here lately."

"I thought La-La Land was bad enough for guns. Now we have to worry about video cameras as well?"

"Video paparazzi," Michael corrected. "Haven't you been watching the hit of the summer—*The Lowdown with Don Lowe*?"

"What I saw was pretty low-down. They not only get embarrassing videos of people, but then make snide cracks about them." Liza rolled her eyes. "And the biggest mouth belongs to Don Lowe. From the way he hogs the camera, it looks as if he wants it both ways, making fun of celebrities while becoming one."

She edged Michael's Honda toward the guard shack while craning her neck to find the jackass with the camera. "Does that mean they wanted a shot of me?"

Michael shrugged again. "Their offices aren't that far away."

"Great," Liza growled as she opened her window to give some ID to the guard, who checked his list for her name. Michael already had a pass. "I'll end up on TV, which adds at least twenty pounds to a person, on a morning when I got up before four o'clock."

"Which adds about twenty years—" Michael broke off

as Liza rammed an elbow into his side. "Well, maybe they won't use it. You're not falling out of your clothes, reeling from an overdose, or punching people out." He rubbed his ribs. "At least they didn't catch you attacking me."

The guard directed Liza to a parking lot near the sound-stage where *D-Kodas* was filming. She pulled into an empty space and then headed for a building that looked like an aircraft hangar. No sooner than Liza announced herself at the heavy door, a production assistant came rushing over to greet her. "Fran Evans," the young woman identified herself. "Great to meet you, Ms. Kelly—and thanks for delivering her, Mr. Langley," Fran added, brushing over-long bangs out of her eyes.

"Glad to do it," Michael replied. "Do you mind if I tag along for the grand tour?"

"I don't suppose it's all that different from any of the film shoots you've worked on," Fran said. "In fact, you'll see less, since there's nothing going on today."

"I'm hoping for a chance to walk on the same stage where Darrie Brunswick sets up the puzzles." Michael put his hand to his heart, doing his best to look like a stage-struck fan.

Fran giggled. "Don't let her hear you talking like that," she warned in a whisper. "She'll believe you."

The PA reverted to more businesslike form. "The rest of our early visitors are enjoying a light collation in the script room."

Translated, coffee and bagels, Liza thought. Not the greatest breakfast, except that her stomach gave off a loud growl at the thought of it.

"Just this way," Fran said, leading them behind the game show's set, down a hallway, and into a crowded room.

Well, more people came in to get oriented than I expected, Liza thought. *Maybe the producers are offering something better than bagels.*

Actually, they had croissants. Liza snagged one, grabbed

a cup of tea, and turned to scan the room. She quickly spotted Will Singleton, even though he was shorter than almost everyone else in the room. America's most famous sudoku exponent was chatting with Wanda Penny, the syndicated acrostics columnist. Will brought his head back and laughed, showing off a beard that was more white than salt-and-pepper.

Will was very proud of his facial foliage, but Liza thought it made him look like Papa Smurf—except that Will had apparently been vacationing in the sun—his face was bright red instead of blue. Wanda Penny was laughing with him, her cloud of frizzy hair bobbing in time with Will's beard. With her diminutive stature, big eyes, and chipmunk cheeks, she looked like a cartoon character, too.

Another familiar face came across Liza's field of vision, but this wasn't someone she knew personally. It was just that she'd seen Lolly Popovic growing up on various TV series. Now she was an adult and becoming a real star on *Newport Riche*.

Liza glanced over at Michael and realized his gaze was following the young woman as well. "Hey," she muttered. "Keep that up, and you'll get an elbow somewhere else you won't like."

"Hey, Liza," a cheeky voice greeted her.

Liza turned to encounter a face she didn't want to see. Ritz Tarleton came sauntering up, clicking her cell phone shut, a smirk on her too-sharp, foxy features. "You bring along your hunky blond boyfriend?"

Kevin Shepard, Liza's old hometown flame, was indeed blond and hunky. And he'd been around a lot since she had come back to Maiden's Bay—even accompanying Liza for the sudoku classes at the minimum-security prison where she'd met Ritz.

"I'm afraid you'll just have to make do with Liza's husband." Michael didn't manage to carry that off as lightly as he'd probably hoped. But then, any mention of his romantic rival tended to make him grit his teeth.

"Oh. Oopsy." The young woman's pale blue eyes moved up and down Michael's lanky frame in a frank once-over. "You're pretty hunky, too. What do you do?"

"I'm in the Business." Southern California might have millions of businesses, but only one that got a capital letter—moviemaking. "I did the script for an indie film—"

The slightly predatory gaze Ritz had been giving Michael turned off as abruptly as if a switch had been flipped. She might be little more than a glorified hanger-on in the Hollywood scene, but even she knew that writers were at the bottom of the moviemaking food chain.

Ritz aimed a smirk at Liza as Lolly Popovic walked past again. "That's the one you'll have to worry about. I hear her mom was the original Polish actress who slept with all the writers."

Could she be more insulting? Liza wondered. *Ritz managed to hit the trifecta—Michael, Lolly, and me.*

Lolly must have heard the comment, too. She turned, sweetly saying, "Of course, my mom married an Oscar-winning writer-director—my dad, Lukas Popovic."

"I worked with your mother on a project a few years ago," Michael told the young actress. "She's a real pro."

Ritz aimed a *"What did I tell you?"* look at Liza as she slunk off, pulling out her phone again.

Lolly smiled at Michael. "Really? Mom is around here somewhere." She stuck out her hand.

"Michael Langley," Michael introduced himself as they shook. "And this is my wife, Liza Kelly."

"The puzzle person!" Lolly had apparently studied her briefing materials. "I hope you're not going to make us look like idiots."

"We were told to make the puzzles tough but fair," Liza assured Lolly with a smile.

Lolly brought her voice down. "Could I ask a favor?" she asked, glancing off to the side. "There's someone I want to introduce to you—she's kind of the wallflower at this party."

The actress stepped away and quickly returned with a young Asian woman in the sort of suit Liza would expect to see at the front of a classroom.

Lolly did the introductions. "Sam Pang, this is Liza Kelly and her husband, Michael. Michael is a movie scripter, and Liza—"

"Sudoku. Yes. Of course." The young academic finally found her voice. She shook her head, getting a bounce out of the ponytail she'd pulled her glossy black hair into. "Sorry," she said, her cheeks going pink. "I guess I'm a little too ordinary for all this—this—"

"Might as well get used to it," Michael advised. "Go with the flow. Appearing on a TV show is sort of like being shot from a cannon. Accept that they're going to move you around, and just concentrate on keeping cool."

"Doesn't that sound like fun?" Lolly's infectious grin managed to get at least a slight smile from Samantha Pang.

"Well, I think I've brushed away all my crumbs," came a practiced announcer's voice from near the coffee urn. Liza looked over to see a face familiar both from the tube and from real life. Wish Dudek, the host of *D-Kodas*, aimed a genial smile at the group. "As the official ambassadors for the show, Darrie and I would like to welcome you."

"Hi, everyone." Darrie Brunswick, the show's co-host, looked tiny and a little washed-out without the dramatic makeup and flossy costumes she wore onstage. "We're going to have a little tour of the facilities and a chance to meet the great people who really get this show on the road."

I guess that's better than the "little people" we used to hear about in Oscar speeches, Liza thought. As she and Michael joined the tail end of the group following Darrie and Wish, Liza glanced down at her blazer. Damn. Croissant crumbs.

They stepped onto the show's set, facing raised banks of seats with cameras positioned in the aisles. It was a good size for a soundstage, but the amount of seating was really about the same as she might have found in a multiplex movie theater—one of the rooms showing a less-popular film.

The set itself looked smaller than it did on TV. Instead of the wide-open spaces that Wish and Darrie traversed on the way to the game board, the host's podium was little more than a brief stroll. *Chalk one up for deep-focus lenses on camera cranes,* Liza thought. *Well, maybe the disappointing reality will help Sam Pang get her feet under her.*

She looked around for the young mathematician in the crowd but couldn't spot her. Then Liza realized she'd managed to lose Michael, too. She found herself standing beside Will Singleton and Wanda Penny as the director and head cameraman made brief speeches.

In whispers, Will made introductions. "I'm afraid Wanda is suffering from a bit of sensory overload."

"It's natural," Liza told the acrostics expert as they got to see where the contestants stood, the host's podium— Liza couldn't help but notice the platform built in to make Wish look taller—and Darrie's game screens.

"You'll see that we have a new set for our twenty-fifth year," the director said.

Liza nodded. The show's original set had looked like a cheesy carnival sideshow, and then they had gone Vegas. Now the various consoles and screens wouldn't have looked out of place on the bridge of the starship *Enterprise.*

"And we're building a special section here for our experts," the director went on.

This was a much less impressive construction, more like something Liza would expect to see in a fan film. The stand-up podium didn't have as much of the muted blue neon as the rest of the set. And the arch and doorway behind it weren't even finished, just bare lumber without any flats erected to cover the framing. Most of the visitors still clustered around the contestant area or fantasized about being Wish or Darrie.

Instead, Liza moved behind the console where she would be filmed, noticing that at least the electrical innards had been installed. One of those touch screens with a pen stood ready for experts—she had a hard time considering herself in that category—to demonstrate moves.

She stepped aside when she noticed Will and Wanda had joined her. "I guess we should be glad we're actually on the set," Liza said ruefully. "They could have just shot us somewhere else and cut us in as needed."

Wanda stepped behind the console, peered out at the empty seats, and then stared up at the spotlights set on metal frames above her. "I saw you both on that televised sudoku tournament," she said. "Will told me that you actually had makeup artists working on you."

"They just dusted a little powder on us so no one would see us sweat on camera," Liza joked.

Then she noticed how tightly Wanda's hands gripped the edges of the console.

"I can tell you for a fact that the makeup people here can work miracles," Liza told her. "We hired Gloria Harrigan, the head of the department, when we had to get a client who will remain nameless to the Music Awards after her boyfriend gave her a shiner."

"Was that the case where the police leaked the photo?" Will asked. "What was that girl's name? Jessie Something?"

"You won't hear it from me," Liza said firmly, "except to say that Gloria literally fixed our client's face so she could sit in the audience without looking like an extra from one of those living-dead movies."

She broke off. "Speak of the devil." She stepped over to

the outskirts of the crowd, where a more casual dress code marked the show's tech people. "Gloria? I'm Liza Kelly. You did some work for me and Michelle Markson—"

"Whoa, I remember her," Gloria said, a shudder going through her plump form. She looked more closely at Liza. "And I remember you—the nice one."

Liza quickly explained about the celebrity experts and how it was apparently Wanda's first TV appearance. "If it's not too much trouble, could you let her know what she can expect?"

"Yeah, sure," Gloria replied. "The big shots don't pay much attention to us techie types at these hoedowns. If it weren't for the free croissants, we probably wouldn't turn up."

She followed Liza to Will and Wanda and went through the introductions.

"We'll expect you early for makeup, but it shouldn't take all that long," Gloria assured Wanda. "It's gotten a little crazier since we started shooting in HD, but all of you have decent enough skin. You wouldn't believe some of the people we have to paint up. Do they have pores, or are those extra nostrils?"

She glanced around as the official tour began moving off. "Wanna see my part of the operation?"

They followed the main body down a hallway, but then Gloria went right when the group turned left.

"Right down here," the makeup supervisor said, opening a door. "It's not the biggest—"

She broke off, blocking the way into the room. "What the hell are you doing here?"

2

Liza stepped through the doorway at Gloria's heels but froze just inside as the makeup supervisor had.

Samantha Pang blinked up at the newcomers. She sat in a makeup chair facing them—and away from the large mirrors on the wall. *Maybe that is a good thing,* Liza thought. *Her face . . .*

Someone had been very busy. An extremely pale makeup base had been liberally applied, turning Sam's face almost clown-white. But more makeup had been skillfully applied with just the opposite intention of the usual beautification job—emphasizing all of Samantha's facial flaws. The young academic had slightly wide lips, but a liberal application of bloodred lipstick stretched them almost to her ears. The addition of pinks and yellow to her small nose had turned it into an eruption—a giant pimple ready to pop right in the middle of her face. A thick black unibrow stretched over her eyes, and although the top of her black hair had been left alone, big, foamy masses hung in the hair on either side of her face.

Liza finally tore her eyes from the spectacle to look at the perpetrator—Ritz Tarleton.

"I was just—" The heiress stood with both hands behind her back, but Liza caught a glimpse of Ritz stashing something in her rear pocket. "I mean, Samantha here was kind of worried about going on TV, so I figured I'd show her what goes on here—and maybe change her look a little."

"A *little*?" Liza echoed, unable to keep her eyes from the train wreck that Samantha's face had become.

"Maybe I got carried away a bit," Ritz admitted. "We were just going to lighten her hair a little, so I used this stuff—"

She pointed to a set of bottles on one of the taborets beside the chair.

Gloria swung around. "You used *that*? It's only supposed to be for instant streaks, and a little goes a long way. How long has it been on?"

"Not too long," Ritz said a little nervously.

Sam looked a lot more nervous as Gloria hauled her out of the chair. "We've got to wash that out—now. It's far too strong."

She continued to tug at Samantha's arm, but the young woman had finally seen herself in the mirror and stood rooted to the floor, a little squeak coming out of her throat.

Sam stared at Ritz. "What did you do to me?" A tear gathered at the corner of her eye and dribbled down her left cheek, making a trail through the clownish makeup.

Gloria finally hustled her over to one of those beauty salon sinks with the built-in headrest and began washing out the hair bleach. "Too damaged," she muttered. "It's breaking."

She whipped around, pointing a gloved finger at Ritz. "You—out!" Gloria was a little more conciliatory with Liza. "You'll have to forgive me, but this young lady really needs my attention."

Liza could see that. Splashing water on the makeup job

had only left poor Samantha looking even more grotesque—especially with two uneven wings of bleached white hair flanking the untouched glossy black on the crown of her head.

Hearing a click, Liza turned back to the doorway, but Ritz Tarleton was already gone. Wanda Penny stood in the opening. All the worries that Liza had hoped to allay stood out more clearly on the puzzle maker's face as she unconsciously patted her mouse brown, frizzy curls. "I don't think this is a good idea," Wanda said faintly, staring at Samantha.

Liza could only sigh. "Let's see if we can catch up with the official tour," she suggested.

Since we've had so much fun with our personal, behind-the-scenes look, she added silently.

After wandering down three dead ends and giving Wanda two assurances that they'd witnessed a freak accident, Liza got them onto the tail end of the larger group. Wanda immediately made a beeline for Will. One look at his jittery friend, and he shot Liza an exasperated look.

Liza had time for only an apologetic shrug before Michael showed up beside her. "Where were you?" he demanded in a whisper. Then, as he took in the expression on her face, he added, "Do I want to know?"

"I stumbled across Ritz Tarleton playing head games—literally—on Samantha Pang," Liza told him.

"I can't believe an innocent flower like our dear Ritz would be up to no good." Michael's sardonic grin belied his pious phrasing.

Liza told him what she and Wanda had found in the makeup department as they trailed along behind the tour. *Boy, I hope they're not saying anything I really need to hear,* she thought as she finished her description.

"As for 'our dear Ritz,' the only flower she reminds me of is a Venus flytrap," Liza ended.

"Yeah, she looked pretty willing to eat me up until she blew me off," Michael said.

The tour meandered its way to Makeup, but neither Gloria nor Sam Pang was in evidence. Probably just as well. The poor mathematician wasn't exactly a shining endorsement for the department's skills.

At last, the tour broke up, Darrie Brunswick taking the celebrities under her wing while Wish Dudek came over to the puzzle people.

"I hear we have you to thank for this," Liza said as she greeted him.

"Well, the germ of it came on that plane ride we had together," the host told her, the skin around his eyes crinkling as he gave his trademark mischievous grin. "The powers that be like to start each season with a Celebrity Week." He shot another grin at Liza. "It's great publicity. So I thought, if celebrity contestants were good, celebrity puzzle artists would be better."

"I never considered myself an artist," Wanda Penny said.

Liza didn't answer, because most of her attention was on the statuesque woman kissing Michael.

Will followed her gaze. "Isn't that your husband?"

"Supposedly," Liza replied, walking over.

Michael broke the lip-lock just in time to see Liza arrive. "Oh, Liza, er . . . this is Rikki Popovic. Rikki, my wife, Liza."

The woman turned around. Close up, Liza could see this Rikki had a good fifteen years on her—and still had impressive cleavage.

"It's short for Ulrica," she said, shaking hands. "Your husband is a very talented man."

Michael colored a little. "I mentioned that Rikki worked on a picture I scripted."

The name finally registered—along with Ritz Tarleton's catty comment about Rikki Popovic sleeping with writers.

Rikki evidently misinterpreted the look. "Nowadays my reputation pursues me," she said. "Back home in Poland, I was Ophelia in *Hamlet*. Coming to America, my English wasn't so good, but my boobs were." She gestured to that cleavage, revealed in a low-cut purple sweater. "That was how I got work."

She sighed. "Now my English is fine, but I don't get work playing sexy girls anymore. The sexy girl's mother, sometimes the sexy girl twenty years later . . ."

"At least your daughter might have a different career," Liza said.

Rikki Popovic's full lips pursed. "I didn't even want her in the Business. We saved up all the money she made for college. And then she says she wants to put it off because of this show she's in."

"Well, it led to a movie deal, didn't it?" Liza shrugged. "I read about it in *Variety*—Stanley Lumiere's latest project, where just about every actress under thirty was angling for the lead."

From the expression on Rikki's face, she'd heard that a little too often lately. "You know how quickly those deals, even Stanley's, can turn into thin air," she replied. "How frequently."

She paused for a moment. "You work with Michelle Markson, don't you? I wonder if you would mind having dinner with Lolly and me. Maybe you could speak to her—"

Liza blinked. "But you have more years in the Business than I do—" She broke off. That might not have been the most tactful way to put it.

"What I had—have—is a B-movie career," Rikki said flatly. "That doesn't match Lolly's . . . dreams. But you—your agency—you deal with the big shots. You can explain what it's really like."

"I don't know . . ." Liza glanced over at Michael.

"You were ready to help your friend Derek's niece." Michael shrugged. "Rikki is a friend of mine."

I'm just not sure I want to know how good a friend, Liza thought. Aloud, though, she gave in. "Okay, I suppose."

"I can book a table for four at Villanova, the new Northern Italian place." Michael dug out his cell phone.

"Let's tell Lolly." Rikki Popovic led the way to the group around Darrie Brunswick.

"We arranged a nice place for you to hang in between tapings," Darrie was saying to Lolly.

"'Hang?' What is this, the Sensational Sixties?" Ritz didn't even bother to lower her mocking voice.

But that changed at Darrie's next words. "It's the Boots Bungalow."

"Baby Boots?" Lolly looked up in surprise. "The child star from the thirties?"

"The very same," Darrie replied. "She was a big star for Mammoth. The studio built special accommodations—"

"Wait a minute," Ritz interrupted. "Why does *she*"— she pointed at Lolly—"get a perk like that? You think she's the only star around here?"

Darrie looked down her nose at the heiress. Liza had to agree. Ritz had "starred" on the cable travel show underwritten by her dad's tourism company. And even then, her participation came down to running around in a bikini saying, "Is this cool or what?"

Then there was the CD where each cut sounded like an outtake from Britney, or Jessica, or any other blond singer.

As for Ritz's movie stardom, she'd played the bitchy girl who got killed off in the first fifteen minutes of a horror flick.

But Lolly Popovic responded with a conciliatory hand wave. "Is there enough room to share? I think I'd prefer a roommate."

Ritz was so surprised, she didn't even try to demand more. Rikki Popovic separated her daughter from the group and explained about dinner with Liza and Michael.

Lolly's face radiated enthusiasm. "I'm so glad! I have

so many questions—you did such a great job of launching Jenny Robbins's career—"

"I wouldn't exactly look at it that way." Liza tried to keep her voice light, but there was a lot of pain underneath. Jenny was the niece of an old friend, and yes, her debut film, *Counterfeit*, had opened to critical and financial success, prompting a lot of other movie offers. But most of Liza's publicity work for Jenny had involved managing the media coverage of some pretty traumatic events for the girl—murder, suspicion of murder, kidnapping, mind games from one of the directors on the film . . .

"Jenny went through some ugly times," Liza finally said.

"But now some of the biggest directors in Hollywood want to cast her for their projects," Lolly said.

"And that makes it all worthwhile?" Michael had seen some of what Jenny had gone through, and he obviously didn't think so.

"Well, there'll be a lot to discuss over supper," Rikki Popovic spoke up.

"I made a reservation for the first seating." Michael looked at his watch. "Can't go too late—I've got to be on set early in the morning."

Liza sighed. "Don't we all."

The next morning, Liza dragged herself out of her hotel bed. All too often when she had to get up early, she'd end up squinting over at the alarm clock about every two hours, making sure she wasn't oversleeping. So instead, she was spending her second day sleep-deprived and groggy.

Moving clumsily, Liza got dressed and headed down to the lobby to meet her fellow puzzle experts. Blessedly, Will had gotten hold of a few cups of coffee. Liza sipped at hers until the car from the studio arrived. They moved smoothly through the studio gate—at this time of day, there were no lurking paparazzi, video or otherwise. When Liza and the others came into the soundstage, staffers immediately whisked them off to Makeup.

Liza found herself taking a seat from Samantha Pang—well, they had similar complexions. The Kelly name may have come from her father, along with a chestnut tinge in her shoulder-length dark hair. But the rest of Liza's looks came from the other side of the family, the Watanabe side.

"You look great," Liza told Sam—and she meant it. A very short gamine cut brought out the fine bone structure of the mathematician's face.

Sam, though, looked as if she'd just bitten into a piece of rotten fruit. "This is as much as they could save since most of my hair just broke off. And then they had to dye what was left."

Obviously she was still struggling to get over what Ritz had done to her.

With his sunburn, Will was destined for the attentions of Gloria as well.

"Only the best for people with *special* skin tones," a young African American guy said from the chair next to Liza. She had a little difficulty recognizing the rapper Forty Oz. without his ton of gold jewelry. "For me, you see, the lighting's a difficulty." He put extra emphasis on the last syllable, as if he were performing. "Make it too bright so people can see me, and the white folk look kinda washed-out."

His sharp, intense features tightened in a mirthless grin. "Got to make sure I don't fade back into the shadows."

"Like that's going to happen," Gloria scoffed. "I never heard anyone call you 'wallflower.' "

Liza submitted to the ministrations of the makeup artist, getting the works—a base coat of pancake, highlights, toning, even work around her eyes. Soon enough, she was declared ready and directed to the greenroom.

She found several people already sitting around. Liza spotted Samantha Pang working on a sudoku, of all things.

So was Lolly Popovic, looking somewhat subdued. Liza hoped that wasn't the result of their dinner-table conversation last night. Both the young actress and her mom seemed so intent on establishing what Lolly called a "legitimate career" that Liza had to warn against loading too much importance onto this single film deal.

Lolly angrily crumpled up her puzzle. So did Sam.

Liza didn't say anything—out loud, at least. No sense in ratcheting up the tension for two of the contestants.

I just hope this isn't a sample of how they'll act in front of the camera, Liza thought.

Fat chance.

3

Waiting for the cue to make her entrance, Liza shot a dubious look at the doorway she was supposed to pass through. The *D-Kodas* set always looked so solid on TV. Seen from behind, this entrance seemed held together with staples and spit.

One of the stagehands preparing to slide the doors apart caught her look. "Hey, we had to get this ready ASAP," he whispered. "We'll hold it steady. Trust us."

Liza rolled her eyes. Those last two words represented the biggest red flag known to show business.

She didn't have a chance to comment, though. Wish Dudek introduced her, and the stagehands slid the doors open. Liza had to admit, they worked together so smoothly, the jerry-rigged entrance never moved.

Then she had other things to think about, like not blinking from the brilliant spotlights facing her—or flinching at the rush of applause from the barely seen audience. She only wished the camera was equally hard to spot.

"Well, Wish," she said brightly, walking to the mark on

the floor that she was supposed to hit. "For this round, contestants will tackle a simplified sudoku. Instead of a nine-by-nine grid, this is four-by-four." Off to the side, the main puzzle board lit up, revealing the puzzle.

"The rules are simple," Liza went on. "The grid can break down into four rows, four columns, or four subgrids, each with four spaces." As she spoke, she used the light pen to outline a row, a column, and a subgrid.

"Based on the clues given, contestants must fill each of those subdivisions with the numbers one through four—with no repetitions."

Wish picked up the spiel. "Now, for purposes of this round, notice the two spaces outlined in red."

The borders on two spaces toward the middle of the grid suddenly changed color.

"Now pick up your signaling devices," Wish told the six contestants. "The blank spaces will light up randomly. If you believe you have the correct number to fill the space, ring in. Everyone ready?"

The empty spaces on the puzzle began to light up. Claudio Day was the first to ring in—the star quarterback's

gridiron reflexes apparently gave him an advantage with the signal device.

Too bad he didn't have the sudoku skills to match. "Two?" he said in a hopeful voice.

"Sorry," Wish said. "We'll continue."

Other spots lit up, including one of the red-rimmed ones. Sam Pang rang in. "One."

Wish nodded. "Correct." The number appeared in that space. "Ten seconds to claim the other."

If she could identify that one, she should know the other, Liza thought.

But Samantha bit her lip and didn't go for the win. The light moved on.

Lolly rang in, correctly identifying a 3 in an illuminated spot.

Another spot lit up. Chard Switzer said, "Oh!" and tried to ring in, but was too late.

Forty Oz. blurted out, "Three!" at the next space, but Wish disallowed that. "You didn't ring in," he explained.

The rapper's face twisted, and he muttered, "Damn!"

Lights blinked their way across the board, but nobody

rang in. Liza began to feel a bit concerned. This wasn't supposed to be particularly difficult. If the celebrities choked on this, how would they do with the higher-level puzzles?

She glanced over at Lolly and Sam, who both stood with their signalers in tensely clenched hands. Liza had seen them working on sudoku. How could they not get this?

The other red-bordered spot lit up, and Ritz Tarleton buzzed in, singing out, "Four!"

"That's correct," Wish said. "Do you—"

The celebutante's voice cut right over his. "It's forty-one."

"Four, one, yes." Wish paused, shooting her a look. "Unless there's anything else you want to add?" His voice was mild with an underlay of sarcasm.

Ritz rolled her eyes.

"Fine, then. As the winner, you get to choose your partner for tomorrow's team round."

"I choose Lolly," Ritz said confidently.

Sam Pang looked a little surprised at this. So did Lolly.

With that, taping broke for a few minutes as Lolly and Ritz both left their places. So did Liza, noticing that the doorway did jiggle when the stagehands didn't have to worry about being on camera.

On the other side stood Wanda Penny, looking as if she were seriously reconsidering the whole idea of being on camera.

"You did so well!" Wanda said, her frizzy hair floating around as she all but jittered in place. "I'm sure I'm going to mess up—babbling instead of explaining things clearly."

Ritz came walking past. She glanced at Wanda and gave a single chuckle that sounded remarkably like the word "loser."

Then she glanced at Liza and raised her foot. "What do you think?"

The high-heeled shoe she wore was just a webwork of leather straps, creating a set of half-inch squares on her feet and up her ankle. "Sudoku shoes," Ritz said, with a condescending glance at Liza's flats.

Before she could move on, Ritz found Darrie Brunswick in her face. "As a guest I'd expect you to show a little respect for your host and not step all over his lines."

Ritz gave the hostess an almost contemptuous look. "You mean stand there like an idiot while he trots out some inane old joke? The director told me we were supposed to keep things moving along."

Darrie flushed under her makeup. "Look here, missy. We've put twenty-five years into this gig and deserve respect just for doing that—"

"Kind of hard to offer much respect to somebody wearing last year's prom gown from a third-rate designer."

Darrie's face went from red to white with rage. *"What?"*

Ritz shrugged. "C'mon, Darrie, you have to know your costumes are famous—and not in a good way."

Liza had to admit that dart definitely hit the target—while also apparently landing on a sore spot for Darrie Brunswick. She started screaming at the younger woman, drawing a worried-looking Fran Evans and then an assistant director.

Ritz faced the abuse with a sweet smile. "I think you're holding up the taping, Darrie, dear."

She turned to Lolly Popovic, who stood looking at her cell phone. "They won't need us for a while. What do you say we head back to that bungalow and chill?"

Lolly's response was more along the lines of a noncommittal grunt as she stared at the small screen on her phone.

I guess I've gotten out of the habit of cell-worship up in Maiden's Bay, Liza thought ruefully. *She must have turned her phone on as soon as they broke taping—not that she's enjoying whatever text message she's looking at all that much.*

Snapping her phone shut, Lolly followed Ritz off the set.

The other girl was already talking on hers. Liza wondered if Ritz had gone through phone withdrawal during her brief prison stint, unable to talk or text.

Even with Ritz gone, Darrie Brunswick hadn't stopped her screaming. In fact, her outrage and complaints just rose in volume—while also rising up the local chain of command.

Finally, the show's director entered the fray. "Darrie, you know how we depend on you," he began.

She cut him off. "Then you depend on this," the hostess snapped, standing nose to nose with her boss. "Either you get rid of that little snot, or you do the show without me."

The man shook his head. "Darrie—"

"From the moment she showed up here, all your precious Ritz Tarleton has done is disrespect us and disrupt the show." Darrie's voice had gone from loud and angry to low and venomous. "Well, if she can do that, so can I. I was doing *D-Kodas* when she was in diapers. No way am I going to let her spit on what we've accomplished."

Whirling on her high heels, Darrie stalked off.

The director stood in silence for a moment, watching her leave. Then he sighed. "I think we may as well take an early lunch. The folks in production will have to take this up."

Production assistants began spreading the news, and in moments, the soundstage had pretty much cleared out.

Liza got her cell phone and called Michael's number. "We've been given an early lunch. Do you think you can get free?"

"Looks that way," he replied. "Our director is in conference with the female lead. They're in his office, and whether they're upright, horizontal, or conferring tantric style, it looks like it's going to take a while. What do you say I come over there and pick you up? Maybe we can sneak off the lot."

"And miss the studio canteen?" Liza teased. "I wanted to see all the stars in costume."

"You're more likely to see extras, and most of them will just be wearing their own clothes," Michael told her. "Just give me a couple of minutes, okay?"

He was as good as his word, arriving behind the set almost immediately. "So how are you enjoying the wonderful world of make-believe?"

Liza grimaced. "Unfortunately, the world of reality keeps pushing in. I expected Sam Pang to kick butt. Instead she seems to be ducking down and lying low. Ritz won the first round, so she's leading a team—and Lolly is her teammate."

"That's not exactly the end of the world," Michael said. "After all, Ritz had a good teacher."

"When I ran that class, she all but blew it off." Liza shook her head in concern. "It worries me that she's the one who won the first round. What does that say about the rest of the players? I'm surprised Will hasn't been coming around to discuss dumbing down the puzzles." She sighed. "Although I don't really know how you could dumb down a four-by-four sudoku grid."

Michael nodded. "You've sort of reached rock bottom already."

Liza spread her arms as if she were trying to reach out for something that eluded her grasp. "It's as if there's a cloud hanging over this whole enterprise, holding everything back."

"We've both been on enough movie sets to know that morale plays a big part in any production," Michael told her. "I've never heard of it affecting a quiz show before, but who knows?"

"It all seems to center on Ritz," Liza fretted. "She's going out of her way to make trouble, and I keep feeling that she's gaming the system—us—everything, somehow."

Michael shook his head. "You can't have it both ways. She can't be a dummy and a master manipulator."

"Really?" Liza asked sarcastically. "I've seen lots of

show-biz egos that didn't have much in the way of smarts, but plenty of low cunning. Certainly, Ritz managed to bring production to a standstill with just a few well-placed remarks. We were supposed to have three shows in the can before lunchtime. If this keeps up, it will take a week to film Celebrity Week."

"Bite your tongue," Michael teased.

"Why?" Liza laughed. "What more can go wrong?"

That was when the earthquake hit.

The first jolt caught Liza off balance, flinging her to the floor. She hit with an "Oof!" and lay still for a second, winded and a little stunned.

Then came a second, deep shaking, not as powerful as the first . . . but strong enough to rattle loose the jerry-rigged entrance. A two-by-six brace popped away from the frame of the doorway, flying back and scything down—straight for Liza's right leg.

She had no time, no chance to get out of the way. The heavy plank landed just below her knee. The world went white as sudden, crushing pain shot from the point of impact, so intense that Liza found herself gulping back sudden nausea.

"Ohmigod, are you all right?" Michael knelt beside her to heave the piece of wood out of the way.

"We've got to get out of here," Liza said weakly. "Go to a—" She broke off. Like anyone who lived in Southern California, she'd had earthquake safety pounded into her head—like looking for a doorway to shelter under.

Hell of a lot of good that did me, she thought.

She struggled to sit up, wincing at another blast of pain from her knee. But when Michael tried to help her rise farther, Liza got light-headed—everything around her seemed to acquire a foggy radiance. She grimly clung to consciousness.

"Can't," she muttered, squeezing her eyes shut.

"Hey! Anybody! I need some help here!" Michael yelled.

With her eyes still shut, Liza heard hurried footfalls.

"That beam fell on my wife's leg." Michael tried to sound calm, but Liza could hear the quiver in his voice.

"Let's get her out. One more shake, and those lights are going to go," another voice said. Hands gently formed a sort of seat under and around her, but Liza let out a gasp as her rescuers raised her up, letting her leg dangle. As smoothly as they could, they hustled her outside, where she could hear confused shouting . . . and a few screams.

When they placed her down, she gritted her teeth to keep from adding some noise of her own. Michael knelt beside her, supporting her in a sitting posture, her head resting on his shoulder. "It hurts." Liza tried to whisper rather than whimper, but she wasn't sure how it came out.

"Could have been worse," a gruff voice said somewhere overhead. "They managed to quakeproof most of these buildings over the years." The voice got a little softer. "She doing okay?"

"We've got to get that leg looked at," Michael said tightly.

"Here comes some help."

Liza heard a siren coming nearer. She opened her eyes to catch the blurry image of an ambulance pulling up.

"Everyone all right here? Anyone need treatment?"

Several voices asked for aid, including Michael's.

A figure in blue surgical scrubs came over, and Michael explained what happened. Gentle fingers probed Liza's knee, but even so, she reacted with a hiss of indrawn breath.

"No blood, so the skin isn't broken," the examiner said.

Fine, but what about the leg? Liza wanted to say, but she just couldn't summon up the strength for a wisecrack.

"What's this I hear about Liza getting hurt?"

That was a familiar voice—Wish Dudek's.

"Mr. Dudek, we're supposed to be setting up a triage system—"

But Wish didn't want to hear it. In moments, he had used his position to scrounge up some sort of transportation—one of those glorified golf carts used to haul visitors and VIPs around the studio grounds. Liza was carefully deposited in the backseat, where Michael supported her while Wish took them at top speed to the studio infirmary.

Liza clung to Michael as they slewed through a turn onto a treelined street that looked eerily like Hackleberry Avenue. The bungalows here served as suburban exteriors in countless movies while also housing producers' offices, accounting operations, even rest spots for stars.

They came up to the carefully tended magnolias that masked the front of the seventy-year-old miniature bungalow originally built for Baby Boots. Liza had passed the place often when visiting various producers at the studio, enjoying the whimsical gingerbread carving at the roofline. She'd promised herself that someday she'd find some pretext to check the place out.

That wouldn't happen now. The roofline seemed to be gone. Even though it cost her some pain, Liza craned her neck, trying to get a glimpse of the bungalow. But all she saw was a pile of weathered lumber where the little house used to stand.

4

Sighing, Liza lay back in her hospital bed, making herself as comfortable as her injured knee would allow. Wish Dudek had ruthlessly used his pull at the studio to get her examined at the studio infirmary. And Atotori Studios, terrified of a lawsuit, had passed her along to a very select little hospital up in Bel Air.

It was the kind of place that patched up A-listers in between car accidents and rehab or dealt with the results of botched plastic surgery. They were used to the demands of their select patients, so they hadn't been that surprised when Liza insisted on having her trousers removed rather than cut off.

"This is Oscar de la Renta," she'd told them. So, even at the cost of a little pain, she'd managed to save her designer pants.

After X-rays and further examination by an orthopedist, she got the verdict—not a broken leg, but what the doctor called "traumatic patellar tendonitis." The area just south of her knee had suffered deep bone trauma. It might not be broken, but it would definitely hurt for a good long while.

So now she lay in a private room with the bottom of her hospital bed raised up and an ice pack on her knee, enjoying a painkiller buzz. The main pain, really, was the news that when she did get out of bed, she'd have to use a walker. "You can't put any weight on the injured leg," the doctor had told her. "In a few weeks, you'll graduate to a cane."

Liza had managed not to tell him where he could put that cane.

Well, the problem of getting around could wait until tomorrow. For now, Liza was content to drift.

The phone rang, but Michael answered for her.

"You have visitors," he announced. "Will and Wanda."

Michael stepped out, and Liza's puzzle compadres came into the room.

Will held out a sheaf of papers. "I worked up a selection of sudoku for you, varying the toughness from slightly distracted by pain to completely drug-addled."

		3	4		8	7		
6			5					
9				1			3	6
	9	8				3		
5								1
		2				9	4	
8	7			3				2
					1			3
		1	7		2	8		

Liza laughed. "Maybe semi-addled," she admitted as Will sorted out some of the puzzles and gave one to her.

"Could I hold on to this?" she asked.

"You can have them all." Will put the sheaf of puzzles on her bedside table.

"I'm really sorry about your leg," Wanda spoke up a little shyly.

"You should be glad," Liza told her. "If Ritz hadn't set off Darrie the way she did, that quake would have hit right in the middle of taping."

"While I was standing under that doorway that fell apart." Wanda looked a little faint now.

Liza gave her an encouraging nod. "And here you were all worried about blowing your lines."

"I think that's the medication talking." Will took Wanda by the arm. "Besides, our time is up."

Liza blinked. "What is this, the Intensive Care Unit?"

"No, but there's a backlog of people who'd like to see you," Will explained as he and Wanda left.

Then the next shift of visitors arrived. Michelle Markson had to hop upward to perch on the side of Liza's bed, aiming a piercing stare down at Liza. With her diminutive size and fine features, Michelle looked like a malevolent pixie. Her companion, Buck Foreman, could have made two of her and could probably have boosted her onto Liza's bed with one hand.

He wouldn't have done that, though. Buck was a former cop, big, buff, and tough-looking in his mirrored sunglasses. But he also had a well-developed sense of self-preservation and knew that any attempt at giving Michelle a hand came at the risk of losing the same.

"Well," Michelle said, "from the look on your face, this whole adventure wasn't as bad as I'd heard."

"The beam fell on my knee, not my face," Liza told her business partner.

Buck took off his sunglasses and looked at Liza closely.

"Dilated pupils," he said. "Guess we shouldn't be surprised. A joint like this, I suppose every white coat is a Dr. Feelgood."

"Given your body chemistry, I suppose I can overlook your tone." From the expression on Michelle's face, she was just managing to keep her famous temper in check.

Liza couldn't care less. She was busy concentrating on something that had drifted up from her memory. "When Wish was rushing me off to the studio infirmary, we passed the bungalow where Lolly Popovic and Ritz Tarleton were staying. I think it had collapsed."

She looked over at Michelle, who had information resources the Pentagon might envy.

"That's as good a description as any," Michelle said. "Ms. Popovic was found unconscious with a bloody gash on her head several blocks away. Apparently, the facade had slid off one of the buildings there, catching her. As a matter of fact, she's being treated in this hospital."

"Where the elite meet to heal." Buck's deadpan delivery made it hard for Liza to decide whether he was joking or not.

Shrugging, Michelle went on. "As for the ever-popular Ms. Tarleton, crews are going through the wreckage of the Boots Bungalow. With her appetite for low publicity, she's probably hiding next door waiting to make a dramatic entrance when the TV cameras arrive."

"I hope that's so," Buck said. "I spotted Hal Quigley in the lobby."

That drew Liza's attention to him. Quigley was a guy she had seen on TV. "The head of the LAPD's so-called celebrity squad?"

Buck nodded, glancing over at Michelle. "Any other celebrity types in trouble?"

Michelle's normally petulant expression turned downright dangerous. "Not that I know of." Her tone suggested that if Quigley knew otherwise, heads would roll in her information-gathering organization.

The bedside phone rang, and Liza fumbled it to her ear. She thanked the person on the other end, hung up, then said, "Seems as though Detective Quigley is coming up to see me."

"Given your somewhat . . . elevated condition, maybe I should stick around," Buck suggested.

"I'd like to hear whatever he intends to bother you about," Michelle added.

Buck sighed. "This isn't some studio flunky, Michelle. We aren't going to find out much if we antagonize him."

"And I imagine that by 'we,' you mean me."

Hearing Michelle say that, Liza braced herself for an explosion. Instead, her partner shrugged. "Probably right. You think he'll let you stay?"

"I'd give it a fifty-fifty chance," Buck said. "We were colleagues but not friends."

"Well, we'll see." With that, Michelle headed out of the room.

A moment or two later, Hal Quigley entered. He was as tall as Buck, but much less bulky, slimmer even than his TV image. After all, the camera added ten to twenty pounds. Quigley's dark hair had the kind of careful styling Liza usually saw on network anchors, and his teeth had her wondering, *Implants or whitening?* His faded blue eyes might have seemed kindly—except for the watchful, probing gaze they directed at her face.

"Ms. Kelly?" he asked.

"Present," Liza replied, "at least physically. Mentally, I'm less sure. They gave me something for the pain in my leg."

Buck Foreman's poker face didn't change, but Liza felt a negative response from him. *Bad move.*

She shrugged. Quigley was bound to find out if he spoke with her long enough.

As if in response to the vibes Buck was giving off, Quigley turned to him. "Hello, Foreman. Guess I should have expected you, considering all the work you've done for Markson Associates since you left the force."

Liza was about to point out that both Quigley and Foreman had essentially the same job—rooting around in the
seamier aspects of celebrities' lives. Then she recalled that
they were supposed to avoid antagonizing the cop.

"So what brings you to my humble hospital room,
Detective?" she asked.

"Ritz Tarleton." Quigley's blue eyes seemed to grow
more intent as he studied her face. "You were one of the
last people to see her."

"Last people? Before the earthquake hit, you mean? Before
it brought down that house—" Liza shook her head. "Wait
a minute. Did I miss something? The last I heard, nobody
knew where Ritz was. Did they find her in the wreckage of
the house? Why would you think something was wrong?"

"She's still unaccounted for," Quigley said.

"So you're apparently investigating a missing person
case—or an accident?" Buck spoke up. "I guess things have
really changed since I left the force."

"Based on information received," Quigley began.

Buck rolled his eyes.

"We heard that Ms. Tarleton might be in danger," the
detective plowed on.

"And I thought I was the one who was medicated," Liza
scoffed. "How many celebrities have used the old 'I'm in
danger' line to get some publicity?"

"We received the information, and now Ms. Tarleton
can't be found," Quigley said. "We also heard that there
was some friction during the taping of the show you were
participating on."

Liza shrugged. "Ritz made herself obnoxious even before
taping began. She showed a lot of attitude to everyone working on the show, crew people, competitors, even the hosts."

"I understand she even made advances on your husband,"
Quigley noted.

"If you know that, why do you need to talk with Liza?"
Buck's voice was suspiciously mild as he asked the question.

"Ms. Kelly was present for an especially violent altercation, and I wanted to hear about it." Quigley turned back to Liza. "That was directly before Ms. Tarleton disappeared."

"Ritz made a catty comment about Darrie Brunswick's wardrobe—which is sort of a national joke," Liza admitted. "But that wasn't the only reason why Darrie exploded. Ritz had been sniping at Wish and Darrie since she arrived on the set—among other people."

She gave him a recital of every miserable bit of business she'd seen Ritz pull during the past day or so. "It's all the kind of mean-girl stuff you'd expect to see in high school, maybe hyped a little because of her celebrity status. But does any of that really leave her life in danger?"

Quigley's phone rang.

"I thought visitors were supposed to turn them off," Buck said in a mild voice.

The cop ignored that as he brought the cell up to his ear. He identified himself, listened, grunted, listened awhile longer, said, "Thank you," and closed the phone.

"They just found Ritz Tarleton," he announced. "It seems she survived the collapse of the bungalow. But as the wreckage settled, it pressed in on her—"

He broke off. "So now I have a warning and a death—either accidental or suspicious. And I intend to find out which."

There didn't seem much more to talk about after that. Quigley left, and Michelle marched in, demanding to hear what had happened. Buck reported while Liza lay back and closed her eyes.

"Don't go to sleep," Michelle warned her. "So, Quigley thinks Ritz was murdered."

Eyes still shut, Liza sighed. Oh, Michelle might turn up her nose when her partner got involved in murder investigations. But Liza knew that the tough-as-nails publicist was a secret mystery junkie, dead set on getting into a case.

"Okay, Michelle," she said. "So who do you imagine is the prime suspect for killing Ritz? She died in an earthquake. Do you figure God finally got tired of her nasty ways and smote her, Old Testament–style?"

"Actually, I'm more interested in that report that Ritz was in danger," Michelle replied.

"Liza called it a cheap way to get publicity," Buck said.

"More like desperate." Michelle gave them a smile as mean as any Liza had seen on Ritz Tarleton. "Maybe it would be worthwhile to throw some questions at the agency handling the late Ms. Tarleton—JSP."

"Jocelyn Squires Publicity?" The words burst from Liza's lips. The Markson/Squires feud was a legend even when Liza started working for Michelle. Jocelyn Squires had been the top associate at Markson Associates, the one everybody expected Michelle to take on as a partner. Instead, Jocelyn had set up her own agency and tried to poach Michelle's clients.

If anyone in Hollywood hadn't known Michelle was ruthless before (that would have to be about three people), the whole Business got the message by the end of this war. JSP never really got up and running. It remained a third-rate operation, trying to drum up coverage for has-beens and folks with more vanity than talent. Using her own connections, browbeating, and probably a little blackmail, Michelle Markson had chased the majority of people off Jocelyn's client list.

"Wasn't JSP the outfit that put up a billboard featuring the rear view of that wannabe actress in a thong?" Buck asked.

"Trust you to remember that," Michelle told him. "Not only was that a desperate idea, but it was recycled. Twenty years ago, another actress took the same billboard—but showing off what she had topside."

Buck shook his head. "A teeny, tiny thong."

Michelle blew out a very loud sigh. "To get your head out of that girl's rear end, I suggest we go over to JSP and ask some questions." She gave Liza a compassionate look that was totally unconvincing. "We couldn't expect you to venture from your bed of pain, darling."

Smiling, Michelle ushered Buck out. A few minutes later, Michael came into the room.

Liza struggled to sit up in her bed. "You've got to get me out of here," she told Michael. "Michelle just announced that she was going to investigate the Tarleton case, and God knows what she'll get up to."

Michael frowned, trying to get up to speed. "There's a Tarleton case?"

"An LAPD detective named Hal Quigley seems to think so." Liza ran through their conversation—or was that interrogation?—about Ritz Tarleton's final interactions. Then she went on to describe Michelle's harebrained idea.

"That could be an interesting interview technique," Michael commented. "'Tell me what I want to know, or you'll never eat lunch in this town again.'"

"It will be a disaster." Liza shuddered. "There's bad blood between Michelle and Jocelyn already. If Michelle goes poking around, we may end up with another dead body to account for."

Michael agreed to put the case to the doctors. Unfortunately, escape wasn't as easy as Liza had hoped.

"The bureaucratic machinery will have to grind until at least tomorrow morning," Michael reported.

Liza nodded. She'd kind of expected that. "I spoke to the *D-Kodas* people. They're still not quite sure what they're going to do, but they said that if I needed it, I could keep my room at the hotel."

Michael gently caught his lower lip between his teeth. He usually did that when he was rehearsing something important to say. "You could stay at the house."

"What house?"

"Our house." He took a deep breath and rushed on. "With that leg, you'll need some help—more, I think, than you'll get from a hotel staff."

"Yeah, all they have is—what? Three stars? What have you got?"

Michael shrugged and managed a nervous smile. "The personal touch?"

Liza shook her head. "I hope this isn't the meds talking, but all right."

The next morning, Liza had a session with the hospital physical therapist, learning how to handle a walker.

"We're giving you a walker with a solid frame," the therapist told her. "It's not as convenient as a folding frame, but it makes up for that in stability."

"It certainly feels solid," Liza said as she worked her way down the hallway.

Michael appeared, Liza signed various papers, and then they headed downstairs. Liza declined the idea of riding in a wheelchair. "I might as well get some more practice in on old Bessie here," she told him.

"Okay," Michael said. "I'll go get the car."

Liza labored toward the entrance while Michael sped on ahead.

Operating this thing is more exercise than I expected, she thought. She was feeling strain not just in her knee, which was unhappy to be moved, but also in her shoulders at the unaccustomed effort of raising the walker and setting it down ahead of her.

Well, older folks humping along on these things didn't make it look like a walk in the park—even when they were walking in the park, Liza told herself.

"Liza!" A voice nearly hissed her name, and Liza laboriously turned around to find Lolly Popovic lurking in the vestibule.

"I heard you were in here," Liza said, looking at the bandage that stretched from Lolly's temple to the side of her forehead. It was about as discreet as a covering for a head wound could be.

Looks as if they didn't have to chop any hair away while patching her up, Liza thought.

But Lolly looked as self-conscious as if the doctors had shaved her head and painted it purple, slouching her shoulders, trying to hide in a lightweight hoodie and sunglasses. "I know they're out there," the girl muttered.

"Who?"

"Paparazzi." Lolly spat it out like a curse word. "I saw the sunlight glinting off one of those monster lenses. Mom's bringing a car, but how am I going to go out there and deal with those—those—"

"Photographers," Liza finished for her. "Well, it's not a stroll down the red carpet. Think of it as an acting job. You've got a prop if you take down that hood. Use the bandage; let them see you in pain. Paparazzi may not have much in the way of human feelings, but you might generate a little sympathy."

Lolly threw back the hood and leaned down to kiss Liza on the cheek. "Thanks, Liza. I really owe you."

"You can work that off right now if you'll just open the damned door." Liza rattled her walker. "It's a little tough handling the logistics with this thing."

"Sure." Lolly pushed the door open, then said, "Oh, here's my ride."

"And here's mine, too." Liza stumped forward as she saw Michael's Honda pulling up behind a hired Town Car. She kept her head down, concentrating on piloting the walker rather than watching Lolly's performance.

And it was a performance, because as soon as the girl stepped outside the door, cameramen seemed to appear out of the woodwork.

"Lolly!" they cried. "How ya doin'?"

"How's the head?"

"Have they given you meds?"

"Lolly!"

"Lolly!"

"Lollylollylolly!"

Liza had to dodge a couple of morons with cameras, but at last she reached the car. Michael already had the back door open, and Liza sank back into the seat, wincing at a sudden lance of pain from her knee. She carefully used both hands to help move her hurt leg inside, and Michael shut the door, tossing the walker onto the front passenger seat and getting behind the wheel. By the nervous glances he shot over his shoulder, Liza saw he wanted to get away as quickly as possible from the mob of paparazzi crowding around the Town Car. Liza clicked her seat belt, sighing with relief as Michael edged the car around the photographers and cameramen, pulled into traffic, and made their escape. She rested back in her seat and shut her eyes for the trip to Westwood, wondering if she was doing the right thing—not just going back to her home, but leaving the hospital. Liza felt surprisingly tired, not just from the up-and-down nonsense with the walker, but also from the fragile way she felt as those photographers heedlessly darted around her. She really, really hadn't wanted one of them to crash into her, terrified of how her knee would feel if she took another tumble.

But there are people who go out every day on walkers, she thought. *I guess Mrs. H. knows what she's talking about when she says old age ain't for sissies.*

They arrived at the little white house—not much more than a bungalow, Liza realized—where she and Michael had lived as husband and wife. A lot of those years had been fun, sharing pleasurable discoveries and companionable silences trying to solve Will Singleton's latest sudoku. Later on, the quiet became tenser as Liza's career outstripped Michael's. Freelancing on series novels and working as a script doctor on straight-to-video movies was all right for starting out, but Michael couldn't make it to the next level. When Liza got promoted to partner, the silence became deafening . . . and they started living apart.

Michael helped Liza from the car, bringing her walker around. As they got to the door, it opened and a cleaning woman came out.

"I figured it was better to bring in some professional help," Michael said with an embarrassed smile.

They entered the living room, where the furniture had been polished until it shone—even the bookcases. Liza noticed that plenty of gaps still showed where she'd removed her books from their joint library. Someone— Michael? The cleaner?—must have pressed knickknacks from all over the house into service to fill the spaces. Liza recognized a few wedding gifts that had stayed boxed in the garage since she and Michael had returned from their honeymoon.

"We moved a bed into the office and made sure you had a clear shot at the bathroom," Michael went on as Liza maneuvered her walker to the couch.

She looked up. "Where are you going to work?"

"Anywhere I have to," he responded with a serious look, then ruined it by grinning. "They set up a place for me at the studio. Which is pretty good, considering that the script seems to change from shot to shot."

"So, do you have to go back to work now?" Liza tried and failed to keep a note of anxiety out of her voice.

Michael shook his head. "We're on hiatus right now. It seems the female lead's husband visited her on the set and interrupted an extremely intense session between her and the director. Apparently the producer has to decide who stays and who goes, so I'm going to be around."

He got Liza settled on his recliner. "I checked it out," he said. "This will actually keep your knee higher than your heart, and that's what they want you to do—rest, ice, compression, and elevation."

With that, he hustled into the kitchen and returned with large bag of frozen peas. "I figured we could use these, since ice tends to melt."

Liza shot a quizzical look at the bag as Michael wrapped it in a towel and applied it to her knee. "I know you hate peas. That's not the bag I left in the freezer when I moved out, is it?"

"C'mon, Liza, the peas would have frozen into a solid lump by now. I got rid of them."

"Exactly when?" she asked.

"Ummmm . . . yesterday?" Michael admitted with a shrug.

Shaking her head, Liza laughed. "I can live with that. Just don't tell me we're having pork chops for supper. I put them in the freezer the same day as the peas."

"I thought maybe we could have dinner at the hotel where you were staying," Michael suggested, "after we pick up the stuff from your room."

"Sounds good to me. We'll just chill for a while—"

The ringing of the phone interrupted her. Michael answered, then handed the receiver over to her.

"Liza?" She recognized Wish Dudek's distinctive voice immediately. "Are you settling in there okay? Personally, I think you should have taken full advantage of the producers and the studio, staying in that hotel and living on room service. Did you know they were debating getting you a nurse?"

Liza rolled her eyes. "Just what I need. Besides, I couldn't really relax, sitting in the lap of luxury when I hadn't earned it."

"Someday you'll have to do something about that annoying independent streak," Wish told her.

"In the meantime, what are they deciding to do about Celebrity Week?"

"The powers that be are going over the footage that

was shot, seeing whether there's enough to do some sort of memorial for Ritz Tarleton," Wish told her. "Otherwise, I think they're going with twenty-five years of *D-Kodas* memories instead."

He paused. "They are checking schedules to see how soon they can reorganize with the celebrities. Claudio Day has an exhibition game, but most of the others will be in or around L.A. in the near future."

"I guess I'm not going anywhere fast." Liza let out a low, annoyed sigh.

"That knee hurting you?"

"No. I've got a dog at home, and a dog-sitter who expects me to collect my pooch tomorrow. Guess I'd better give her the bad news."

Liza rang off with Wish and dialed up Mrs. H. Her neighbor was shocked to learn of Liza's mishap—and way too happy to hear that Liza was staying with Michael.

"Well, I certainly couldn't stand in the way—"

Of true love, Liza grumpily thought.

"Of your recuperation," Mrs. H. went on. "I'd be glad to take care of Rusty. He's a good dog."

From the background, Rusty let out a loud bark on hearing his name . . . followed by a louder crash.

"Up till now." Mrs. Halvorsen sighed.

Liza ended that call shaking her head.

She looked up to see Michael hovering over her like an over-attentive headwaiter. "Do you want to catch a little sleep, or would you—"

The phone rang again.

Michelle's voice crackled over the line, elaborately matter-of-fact. "Jocelyn was getting ready to cut Ritz Tarleton loose."

"How far into your jolly reunion did that pearl of wisdom pop up?" Liza asked.

"Pretty quickly. I wasn't about to stick around that rat hole of an office one second more than necessary." Michelle's claws showed for a second, even over the phone. "I have a few things to take care of at the office. Buck and I can be in Westwood around dinnertime. We'll bring the eats."

"But—" Liza wasn't sure Michelle even heard that. The phone was already dead in her ear.

She looked up at Michael. "Maybe we should head over to the hotel now," she began. "I'll explain on the way."

When they returned, Michael carried Liza's bag, while Liza moved as if the weight of the world had settled on her shoulders. She dropped onto the couch, shrugging repeatedly in an attempt to stretch the muscles. "We've got a little time before Michelle and Buck turn up. Do you want to watch some TV?"

"Sure." Michael handed her the remote and then headed for the kitchen. "I'll get the peas for your knee."

Liza began surfing through channels. The local TV lineup had changed since Liza was down here last. Lots of new syndicated shows turning up—

Her finger froze on the channel button when she spotted a face she recognized—hers.

Liza blinked, realizing this was the front entrance of the hospital where she'd stayed. And there was Lolly Popovic, holding the door.

"So who's that?" a voice off camera asked. "Lolly's grandmother?"

The scene shifted to the motley crew of staffers from *The Lowdown with Don Lowe*. The boss man, Lowe himself, stood in front of a blue screen with the image frozen, arms crossed over his burly chest, shooting an aggravated look at his underling. "Who cares? At least it shows Lolly has good manners."

5

Buck and Michelle arrived soon after Liza clicked off the television. But when Liza complained about her brush with *The Lowdown*, her partner didn't join in her indignation.

"You were standing beside Lolly Popovic, and you knew paparazzi were stalking her," Michelle said. "What did you expect?"

"I didn't expect some jackass on TV to call me a grandma," Liza growled. "Where do they come off doing that?"

"It's the new wave of celebrity news." Michelle's voice got a bit flatter. "Thank Don Lowe for that."

"Who is this Lowe character, anyway?" Michael asked.

Michelle shrugged. "Believe it or not, he started out as an investigative journalist."

"Before he went over to the dark side?" Liza said.

"Actually, he was sort of a crusading investigative journalist for several papers across the country."

Michelle pulled a face. "Yes, there was a time after *All the President's Men* when going into journalism was like joining the Peace Corps." She made a dramatic gesture. "Go forth and write the truth."

"I'll bet it seemed like a steady job," Michael offered. "People would always read newspapers."

"Until the Internet came along," Michelle finished. "Lowe found himself laid off. But unlike most of his jobless colleagues, he didn't start gassing away on public affairs with a blog. He looked for a market with some growth potential—and found it with the public's insatiable interest in celebrities."

"Growth?" Liza scoffed. "There aren't enough tabloids?"

"Not many that have credibility," Michelle answered. "There's no dealing with the ones that run stories about women having Elvis's alien child. But they get away with that kind of nonsense, rumor, and innuendo because people don't take them seriously. The tabloids that count try to run a serious news operation—sometimes they even break real stories before the traditional media pick them up. Those are the ones people pay attention to—and unless it's a really bad story, they can be controlled."

Liza looked at Michelle when she said that. *Translation: I can control those tabloids,* she thought.

"Whatever stories they manage to dig up or buy, the big tabloids need interviews with the stars to make their circulations profitable," Michelle explained for the benefit of Buck and Michael. "Our control of access to celebrities prevents the worst excesses."

She shook her head. "What Lowe did was create a new paradigm—a new market for out-of-work or wannabe journalists, photographers, paparazzi, even civilians with videocams or cell phone cameras. Catch a celebrity in an unguarded moment, get a paycheck. He doesn't need the goodwill of the celebrity, or even a press release. And considering the way most celebrities act when they don't have handlers—and that includes our own clients, I'm afraid—they provide plenty of fodder for snide comments."

"I know the website was so successful it spawned the TV show," Michael said. "But I keep wondering whether

Lowe isn't going to kill the golden goose. If he brings celebrities down to the level of the folks at home, doesn't that kill the magic?"

Michelle shrugged. "Maybe it's the appeal that Jerry Springer had—or those court shows where yahoos missing a couple of teeth wrangle over who totaled the family car."

"Some people just like watching train wrecks," Liza said.

Michael grinned. "There's an idea—Train Wreck TV. Maybe I should work up a proposal and circulate it among the cable networks."

"It won't garner you as much cash or notoriety as Lowe has gotten," Michelle told him. "The website alone has generated so much ad revenue that he's able to buy stories that the big syndicated gossip shows wouldn't dare touch—and he's killing them in the process. Why do you think they're drumming up all these phony controversies these days?"

"Still, I wouldn't mind wiping that smirk off Don Lowe's face," Liza said.

"You and about half of Hollywood," Michelle dryly replied. "Let's get the food out and discuss the case."

Liza wanted to tell her partner that there was no case, but there was no talking to Michelle when she was in this kind of mood. Instead, she just passed utensils around while Buck opened several buckets of surprisingly spiced roasted chicken. From the sauces and side dishes, Liza deduced the food had a Middle Eastern origin, but that was as far as she got.

"A new fast-food discovery?" she asked Michelle.

"Actually, Buck found the place, but I've sworn him to secrecy. We'd like to enjoy the food for a while before everybody starts getting it and the lines are twice as long."

Liza glanced over at Buck, wondering for about the thousandth time exactly what kind of relationship the big ex-cop and her razor-tongued partner shared.

After eating her fill, Michelle leaned back and took a sip of beer. "Now, on to what dear Jocelyn told us."

"Was she really going to cut the cord on Ritz?" Liza asked. "I'd have figured she had to be Jocelyn's biggest client."

"Maybe she was just too high-maintenance," Michael suggested.

Michelle shook her head. "No amount of maintenance was going to keep Ritz Tarleton out of the junkyard. It's amazing she managed to stay in the public eye as long as she did. Although in the last few years, she was more of a joke than a celebrity."

"She was good enough for you to wrangle her into my trial sudoku class at Seacoast Correctional," Liza pointed out.

"You work with what you can get, dear," Michelle responded. "According to Jocelyn, that class managed to create a last-gasp opportunity for Ms. Tarleton. She'd approached Jocelyn about getting on *Celebrity Dance Challenge*."

"Also known as 'Has-Beens in Dance Shoes,' " Michael interjected.

"Exactly," Michelle said. "Learning that the producers of the show considered her too past it to join their collection of dimming stars finally burst Ms. Tarleton's bubble."

Liza nodded. Working with Michelle, she'd often encountered the invisible bubble that formed around the rich and/or famous, insulating them from reality. Often it led to horrendous career and personal miscalculations for celebrities—and, doubtless, golden opportunities for media vampires like Don Lowe.

"Ritz pressed her agent and Jocelyn to find her some sort of high-profile booking, but the best they could do was a backup spot on *D-Kodas*." Michelle glanced over at Liza. "No offense meant."

"None taken." For Liza, the show offered national exposure for her puzzle-making skills. For Ritz, five days on a syndicated game show was a definite downward step—maybe more than one, if she were only an alternate. Just a little farther down, and she'd have ended up the celebrity draw for car dealership openings in the Valley.

"And even that was a last-minute addition because they'd lost a contestant," Buck added. "So the people who were handling her saw the handwriting on the wall. A troublesome client that nobody wanted anymore. After they got the check from *D-Kodas*, that would be the end."

Liza frowned. "Ritz had to know it. So why did she go out of her way to alienate everybody on the set?"

"Maybe she figured she'd go down in a blaze of glory—or at least notoriety," Michael suggested.

"From all her DUIs and shady hookups, Ritz had a pretty wide self-destructive streak," Buck said. "God knows she also had an ego. It's possible she couldn't really believe she was in trouble."

Michelle shook her head in disagreement. "I don't think so. Jocelyn said that when she told Ritz she only had one shot, it was the first time she saw an honest reaction from her client—fear. Ritz was scared."

"So you think she was up to something during the taping of the show?" Liza asked.

"I have no idea," Michelle replied honestly. "But I think we should find out." A crafty smile crept over her lips. "And I think the first person we should ask is the one who got bumped from the celebrity contestant lineup so that Ritz wound up on *D-Kodas*."

"Who was that?" Michael asked.

"Ummmmmm." Liza racked her brain to remember who had been originally scheduled. "It was a singer . . ."

"Sukey Tupp." Michelle supplied the name.

"The British Bombshell of a couple of years ago," Michael said reminiscently. "Turned up at the Grammy Awards wearing just a Union Jack."

"I remember that," Buck said.

Michelle shot them both a look. "More recently, she came across as the British Burnout," she told them. "It seems success went right to her nose. But she had a comeback album released back in June and seemed to have cleaned herself up. Then, two weeks before taping started for *D-Kodas*, Sukey had a relapse. Of course, the standard rehab stint is twenty-eight days, but my sources tell me that Sukey is signing herself out tomorrow morning."

Liza could only laugh. "Well, Michelle, if the publicity business ever goes south, you could always make ends meet by ratting people out to Don Lowe."

The look on Michelle's face showed that she didn't think that line was too funny, but all she said was, "Let's hope things never come to that."

Then she glanced at Liza's propped-up leg. "So, will you be up—and about—to talk with Sukey tomorrow, or should Buck and I handle it?"

"It strikes me that both you and Buck have businesses to run." Liza looked over at Michael. "You're on hiatus, and it looks as if I'm out of the game for a while. What do you say to asking a few questions? I seem to remember that Sukey and Ritz used to be pretty tight."

She turned back to Michelle and Buck. "Not that I think there's a deep, dark mystery about why Ritz Tarleton died. But you do have me wondering what was on her mind that last time I saw her."

Retreatments looked more like a spa than a drying-out clinic, located near the old artists' colony in Malibu. Liza could hear the surf from the Pacific—and feel the chilly breeze coming off the water. It wasn't even eight in the morning yet, the middle of the night for most party people— and the paparazzi who stalked them. But, according to Michelle's usually infallible sources, this was when Sukey Tupp was checking out of the treatment center.

Liza looked up and down the block. Except for Michael sitting beside her, nobody else seemed to be waiting. *I guess Don Lowe and his minions didn't get this newsflash,* she thought.

The glass door opened, and a young woman stepped onto the street. Liza already had her car door open and the walker in position. She heaved herself upright and began stumping across the street, outdistancing a surprised Michael.

Watching her advance, the young woman called out, "Sorry, luv. I don't think this place has the kind of rehab you need."

"It's you I need, Ms. Tupp." Liza hadn't been quite sure before, but that Cockney accent was the clincher.

Sukey Tupp might be a Brit, but she'd fallen back on the usual Californian idea of going undercover—no makeup and large sunglasses. Liza's memories of the singer's brief glory days left her with an image of a saucy, rounded figure, wearing too-tight jeans and always swaying to an insistent drum backbeat.

Rehab Sukey's cheekbones seemed more prominent and the rest of her seemed skinnier . . . or maybe just drawn.

She sighed. "Well, you got me, luv. Should I be smiling for the cameras?"

"I'm not looking for an interview," Liza said. "My name is Liza Kelly—"

Sukey's face actually showed some animation. "The sudoku lady!"

Liza nodded.

"I love those pieces you do in the newspaper," Sukey went on with enthusiasm. "Wherever I go, I try to get the *London Times*—they have the real fiendish puzzles—the *Guardian*, and the local paper that has your column."

I bet her people have an easier time getting hold of the British papers than finding my stuff, Liza couldn't help thinking.

"Thanks," she said aloud. "You sound like a real sudoku fan. I imagine you'd have done well on *D-Kodas*."

At the mention of the show, the singer's face went tight again. "P'raps I might have done . . . 'cepting for my wee indiscretion. You don't really want to hear about that, do you?"

"No, we're hoping you can tell us a little about Ritz Tarleton," Michael said, joining them. "My wife was one of the last people to talk with her before the earthquake."

Sukey's shoulders slumped a little. "I heard about that. Hell of a thing. Some of the people down here on the farm didn't even feel the ground move. It's one of the reasons I decided to leave the place. Not the earthquake or the people—I'm trying to make up my mind whether I want to go to the funeral."

"I thought you and Ritz were pretty close," Liza said.

Sukey jerked her head around. "So why did the dizzy bitch ship me, then?"

Michael had the better handle on British slang. "You're saying she's the reason you're here?"

"Had to go show me face at some award to-do—only cable, but it's still publicity." Sukey halted, a little embarrassed. "Well, I was really fagged out, and Ritz offered to help me out—a hit of, errrr, Andean pick-me-up powder, if you know what I mean."

She shook her head. "Don't know what they cut it with, but the stuff had the exact opposite effect. Fell out of me seat, not to mention my dress, and wouldn't you know it, there was some bastard there from *The Lowdown* with a camera. So there was no hope of hushing it up. Off I went to restore my chemical balance."

And when you went, they needed another body for Celebrity Week on D-Kodas, Liza thought. Surprise, surprise, Ritz Tarleton turned out to be the next female celeb on the list.

6

While Liza considered other questions to ask, a car finally came to pick up Sukey Tupp. Maybe that was just as well—the singer wasn't in much of a mood to reminisce more about Ritz Tarleton anyway.

That suited Liza. Even if Sukey was a fan, the longer Liza spoke with her, the more she seemed to pick up a tone in the woman's voice, as if someone had stretched a wire almost to the breaking point and kept plucking it.

Liza remembered watching videos of Sukey onstage—she had an intensity to her performance, an ability to communicate a vibe. The problem was, the vibe was now enough to make Liza quiver, too.

Methinks Ms. Tupp is not as together as she tries to present herself, Liza thought.

Watching Sukey's attempt (and failure) to maintain her facade made Liza wonder if Ritz had been doing the same thing—only more successfully—on the set of *D-Kodas*.

Slogging back to Michael's Honda, she frowned in thought. Liza had gotten a snootful of Ritz Tarleton's attitude and indolence while trying to teach her in that prison sudoku class. She'd certainly been turned off by the way Ritz behaved—was it really just two days ago? It seemed like a week.

The point was, Liza had put her efforts into ignoring Ritz rather than paying attention to her. Even with that nasty little trick on Samantha Pang, Liza had been more interested in the victim than the perpetrator.

What had really been going on behind Ritz Tarleton's smug-looking little fox face? Who on the set might have had a chance to know?

When she got back to the car, Liza called Buck Foreman on her cell phone. "I imagine Michelle had you checking backgrounds on the major people involved with the *D-Kodas* Celebrity Week."

"Ever since you agreed to take part," Buck told her.

"Did anybody have a history with Ritz Tarleton?"

Buck laughed. "You figure an old enemy stalked her and used the earthquake as a convenient cover-up for doing away with her?"

"I'm just trying to get my head around what she was thinking that last day on the set."

"Mainly she seemed to be thinking about how to give Darrie Brunswick a stroke." Buck chuckled again. "What do you figure? Ritz was planning to take her place and be the new hostess?"

"Unlikely," Liza said dryly. "But she may have mentioned what her plans were if she had a friend on the set."

"I'd say there were two possibilities." Buck rustled some papers together, looking over his reports. "When Ritz started making the whole celebrity scene, she turned up often with the actor guy—Richard 'Chard' Switzer. They were pretty tight, at least to begin with."

He paused for a second. "More recently—within the last few months—Ritz turned up at a lot of places with that rapper guy, Forty Oz."

"Places?" Liza pressed.

"Clubs, hotels, parties . . . and his crib, if you can use that term for a mansion up in Coldwater Canyon," Buck replied. "Papa Tarleton was not happy."

Liza had met Ritz's father. Frederick "Fritz" Tarleton had turned his father's family travel business into a deluxe tourism empire. He'd made a lot of money and had no problems with using it as a weapon.

"Old Fritz hired a beat-down on a former boyfriend who did Ritz wrong," Liza said slowly. "Just how unhappy was he with Forty Oz.?" She thought about the couple of encounters she'd had with the rapper, in makeup and then watching him tape the first game. He had a fast mouth and maybe a temper, not a good combination for dealing with a heavy-handed father.

On the other hand, she couldn't remember Ritz or Forty Oz. even talking to each other on the set. "What's the situation between them now?" Liza asked.

"It seemed to be over, although *The Lowdown* still rehashed some he said/she said stuff about the end of the relationship." Buck sounded almost embarrassed to recount the tabloid gossip. "The Ritz camp says she dumped him, while the other side claims she caught him with a dancer from his touring act."

Interesting point of view, Liza thought, *where infidelity is better than being dumped.*

"As a practical matter, is there anyplace I can catch up with these guys?"

"Forty Oz. seems to be pretty big on the whole entourage thing—I'll have to dig a little to find a reasonably private place where you can get to him," Buck told her. "Switzer doesn't work so hard at being a celebrity. He's got a standing daily appointment at Body by LiComo, which should end in just about the time it would take for you to get there from Malibu."

Liza turned to Michael. "I know where the place is," he said, starting up the car.

"So how does a second-tier comic actor rate a standing appointment at Hollywood's leading body sculptor?" Liza asked.

"It wouldn't be easy," Buck admitted, "except that Switzer was training with Rudy LiComo years before either of them became famous."

"Well, it's nice to see someone displaying a little loyalty," Liza said. "Do you think we'll have any problems getting in there?"

"Nothing that a call from Michelle couldn't take care of," Buck said.

"There's very little in this town that a call from Michelle couldn't handle," Liza told him.

Buck agreed with a not exactly humorous chuckle. Liza said good-bye and cut the connection.

After a quick heads-up call to Markson Associates, Liza sat quietly, just rubbing her right knee as Michael drove on. If she had an ounce of sense, she'd be back home with her leg up and those silly frozen peas soothing the pain. Instead, she was stumbling around on a walker playing detective.

Why? I didn't even like Ritz Tarleton, she thought ruefully. But when she glanced over at Michael, she realized why. He wasn't saying anything, but the tension she saw in his shoulders wasn't from any traffic. He was worried about Lolly Popovic. *And I'm worried about him.* They rode on in mutual, troubled silence until they reached Rudy LiComo's glorified gym.

Michelle had already worked her magic. Not only did they get the red-carpet treatment when they walked in the door, but Rudy LiComo came over to say hello. The head of the gym was a tall, sinewy guy who was losing his hair, so he wore it cut very short.

"Michelle wasn't very clear on what you needed," he said, taking a sidelong glance at Liza's walker. "We aren't set up for physical therapy, although I could make some recommendations. Or are you interested in building some more upper-body strength?"

Liza rattled her walker slightly. "I seem to be getting enough of a workout from this right now," she said. "Actually, I was hoping to catch up with Chard Switzer."

LiComo frowned. "Richie finished his workout. Why don't you go to the juice bar while I pop in the locker room and tell him you're here?"

Getting us out of the way if he decides to leave without talking, Liza thought.

Michael glanced at her, obviously thinking the same thing. Liza shrugged. *LiComo's place, LiComo's rules.* "Great," she said. "I appreciate your help."

The juice bar was more like a miniature Starbucks, located behind the health club's reception area.

Michael took an appreciative sniff of brewing coffee mixed with the scent of cinnamon. "Doesn't quite have the bouquet associated with most of the gyms I've encountered."

"Movie-star sweat isn't all that different from the kind that drips off regular folks." Liza carefully settled herself in a chair and sighed. "Although a place this pricey probably has the last word in air recycling, filters, or whatever."

"Or maybe they just squeeze the celebrity sweat right out of the air and bottle it for the more kinky fans," Michael suggested. He left her laughing as he went to the counter and got two cups of tea. "Earl Grey okay? They mostly had herbal stuff."

"I don't think a little caffeine would hurt." She let the tea brew for a while and then added sugar and milk.

By the time she was finally ready to take a sip, Chard Switzer appeared in the entrance. He came straight toward their table.

Liza pulled the walker a little farther in beside her chair. *Of course, this would give him a good landmark, even if he hadn't met me briefly on the set.*

"You wanted to see me, Ms. Kelly?" Chard asked.

Michael got to his feet and shook hands. "Michael Langley," he identified himself.

Liza decided to get right down to business. "We hoped you'd have a little time to talk about Ritz Tarleton." Either Switzer would open up, or he'd run.

Chard Switzer sat down. "Poor Ritz. She was a piece of work."

That wasn't a response Liza had expected. "I thought you were friends."

"We were," Chard said. "But that doesn't mean she wasn't a piece of work. Ritz gave me my name, you know, even if it was a joke. We were hanging out with the same crowd, both pretty much on the outside, trying to get in."

He shrugged. "I was doing some modeling at the time— jeans, swimwear, beach stuff."

The athletic shirt under his warm-up jacket stretched over a six-pack and impressive pecs.

Michael sat a little straighter, sucking in his gut. He had a lanky frame that developed a bit of a potbelly if he didn't watch himself.

"So, although we both wanted to hang with the cool kids, Ritz and I had different ways. I was eye candy—and arm candy—for the girls. Ritz was always ready to pick up the tab for everybody."

"You managed to earn your way in, getting into the Business," Michael said.

Chard shrugged wide shoulders. "I managed to book a couple of bit parts, enough to earn waivers to get into the union. That's when I discovered there were already actors named Richard Switzer, Rick Switzer, Rich Switzer . . . What was left? These days, Dick has become kind of a joke name."

"Except for controversial Republican politicians," Michael offered with a smile.

"Ritz suggested that I just cut the front off my name," Chard went on, "like Drea de Matteo and Topher Grace." He ducked his head in embarrassment. "It was only after I did it that I found out about the vegetable thing."

"Swiss chard?" Michael said in a faint voice.

Chard nodded. "That was Ritz, making a joke."

"How did you feel about that?" Michael asked.

Chard shrugged again. "Too late to worry about it. And right after I officially joined the union, I got booked for the pilot of *Whack Jobs*. I've been working for seven seasons, so I guess you can say it worked out okay."

Liza frowned. "I'm a little surprised. That doesn't sound like the Ritz I knew."

"Pulling a prank on somebody?" Michael gave her a "What are you talking about?" look. "Compared to what Ritz did to Sam Pang, this name thing seems downright benign."

"It comes across a lot more . . . intellectual than something I'd connect with Ritz Tarleton."

"I've spent years wondering about that." Chard's features, just a squidge off classically handsome, contracted into an almost comical look of perplexity. "It might be like what I do when I play my goofball character."

Liza had seen maybe an episode and a half of *Whack Jobs*, an almost infamously brainless comedy. Chard played Botzu, an immigrant whose most carefully crafted facet was an accent that didn't hook up with any actual locality. It could be but wasn't Spanish, Middle European, Hindustani, or Middle Eastern. He was the eternally clueless, nerdy outsider with inappropriate, outsized reactions to normal American life.

Chard must have seen something in her expression, because he launched into an explanation. "Hey, this isn't a show that works on subtlety. And a lot of jokes about my character—well, if he were female, we'd have the sexism police all over us. It's all, 'Why, Botzu, without your glasses, you're quite attractive—and without your shirt, you're down-right beautiful!' "

"That gender-reversal stuff gets a lot of hooting and hollering from the studio audience," Michael said.

He caught Liza's look and said, "I watch this stuff for research."

Liza turned to Chard. "So you think Ritz spent a lot of time playing dumb?"

"I think there's a certain amount of camouflage involved, that she had more going on than she let people see." Chard spread his hands, shaking his head. "I knew her better than most people, but that's not saying that I really *knew* her."

"Did you hook up with her?" Michael asked.

Chard almost scowled. "I wasn't going to get sucked into that. It was hard enough being her friend. And even though she put the moves on me sometimes, I don't think her heart was really in it. Maybe she knew that screwing would screw the friendship." He shrugged. "Or maybe it was another one of her jokes."

Liza decided to put her question plainly. "Do you think she was joking around on the *D-Kodas* set? It seemed as though she went out of her way to make enemies there."

"And now she's dead," Michael added.

"Ritz seemed more hyper than usual," Chard said. "She used to be a lot more laid-back."

"I hear she was worried about her career." Liza shrugged. "Which may have been a problem, because she didn't actually seem to have a clear-cut career. You sort of said it— Ritz bought her way into becoming famous."

"And now, well, it reminds me of a book I just read, an autobiography of somebody who grew up as well as worked in the Business," Michael added. "What did she say? 'Celebrity is just obscurity waiting in the wings.' "

"I can relate to that," Chard said. "They're saying this

will probably be the last season of *Whack Jobs*—right now, I'm kind of figuring out what to do when I grow up."

Michael and Liza exchanged glances. "After seven years, you've got to be worried about typecasting."

"Oh, yeah," Chard told them. "I turned down a lot of movies during the summer break because most of the scripts I got just reinforced the sort of idiot character I was playing on TV." His face took on a little color. "To tell you the truth, I spent my downtime taking acting classes. I might not end up doing Shakespeare, but I hope I'll be able to tackle a better role than Botzu the Bozo."

"So that's why you wanted to do the *D-Kodas* gig," Michael said, "to show you had something more between the ears than your character."

"That, and I hoped to make a connection with Lolly Popovic." Chard shot Liza another defensive look. "Not like that. I've heard her name mentioned in connection with a couple of big deals. She's going places. And if she were willing to put in a good word for me, even for a small part, I could be heading in the same direction."

Michael looked at him for a long moment. "Well, that's pretty ambitious."

Chard's big shoulders jerked in another shrug. "I thought it was worth a try. But Ritz said not to do it. She told me she was working on something, and if it turned out right, she'd be in a position to make some things happen for me."

Liza leaned forward on the table, ignoring a little throb of pain that came from her injured knee. "Did she give any details about what this 'something' was?"

Chard leaned forward, too. "She clammed up. I was hoping to catch her alone between tapings and maybe find out what she had in mind. But then the earthquake came. Now I guess we'll never know."

"Yeah," Michael said. "Let's just hope it wasn't another of her little jokes."

That was all Chard Switzer could tell them. Liza and Michael thanked him, then went outside the health club to wait for their car.

"A gym with valet parking," Michael muttered as they stood outside. "We are definitely not in Kansas anymore."

"What would you know about Kansas?" Liza asked with a laugh. "You grew up only a couple of hundred miles north of here."

"More like five hundred," Michael corrected her. "And you grew up about seven hundred and fifty, but I thought it was nicer to avoid saying, 'We're not in Maiden's Bay anymore.' "

Liza's cell phone rang before this could degenerate to the squabble level. Resting one hand on her walker, she dug out her phone and flipped it open. "Buck Foreman," she reported, bringing it to her ear. "Have you gotten a line on Forty Oz.?"

"Still working on that," Buck told her. "But I did catch some police gossip. They finished sifting through the collapsed bungalow at the studio. Looks as if Hal Quigley may have guessed right. There's some evidence that Ritz Tarleton's death wasn't quite an accident."

7

"You've got to keep this under your hat, Liza," Buck warned. "I only heard it because an old buddy of mine was on the crime-scene team going over the ruins of the Boots Bungalow."

"Great," Liza said as Michael jerked them along through stop-and-start traffic. "So you're saying this is hot locker-room gossip?"

"It's based on a heads-up on the down-low," Buck replied in annoyance.

"I don't even know if that's anatomically possible," Liza teased.

Buck's voice took on his patented tough-cop tone. "Hal Quigley is taking it seriously—and he's keeping it away from the media."

"So what exactly is it?" Liza asked.

Buck was definitely not in a kidding mood. "When they found the body, it was missing a shoe."

"Okay," Liza said. "Is that necessarily a surprise after an earthquake? I mean, the first shock flung me down."

She shuddered in memory. *And the second nearly cut my leg off.*

"The rescue attempt revealed Ritz Tarleton's body in the middle of the living room. But the crime-scene people turned up the missing shoe in the doorway," Buck reported. "In fact, part of the shoe was caught on the lower door hinge."

Liza remembered the silly footwear that Ritz had been showing off. What had she called them? Her sudoku shoes? Yeah, it wouldn't have been hard for one of those crisscrossing straps to get caught—

She broke off in midthought. Ritz had grown up in Los Angeles, and certainly knew the basic rule about earthquakes and doorways. In fact, the caught shoe demonstrated that she'd *been* in the doorway. So how did she end up halfway back across the room? Could the earthquake really have shifted her that far?

Liza tried to rerun the moment of the temblor through her head. It cast her to the floor and must have loosened the bracing beam that fell on her leg. But could it have really sent Ritz that far from the safety of the doorway? Could she have caught a leather strap on the hinge and still have covered all that distance?

"Judging from your sudden and prolonged silence, you're figuring that it would have to be a much bigger earthquake than we felt to break that shoe and send Ritz flying that far," Buck said grimly. "The only way she could have landed where she did was if Ritz had help—if you could call it that."

Liza sounded just as grim when she spoke. "Ritz made it to the doorway and safety—except someone pushed her back into the house."

"A really serious push," Buck agreed. "Serious enough to break her shoe and send her across the room before the second shock brought the house down on her."

The silence after that exchange stretched long enough

to make Michael turn from behind the wheel of the car. "What's he telling you? Something interesting?"

At the same time, Buck asked, "So does that mean we're giving up on this? Leaving it to Quigley?"

"No—Yes." Liza looked over at Michael. "The 'yes' was for you. From what Buck is saying, it looks as if the cops have solid proof that Ritz didn't die by accident."

"I figured the 'yes' was for me," Buck said. "I know you didn't like the Tarleton kid—hell, she wasn't a kid anymore, was she?"

"No, she wasn't," Liza said into the phone. "Although a lot of people thought she was acting like one. But now I don't think so. She was up to something, and I'd like to find out what."

"You think it may have gotten her killed?" Buck asked.

"We don't know enough even to start guessing," Liza replied. "We'll have to ask some questions, and the first person to talk to seems to be Forty Oz. Are you getting any closer to tracking him down to someplace where we can get at him?"

"He likes to make a splash," Buck said. "I've got some of Michelle's connections working to get a line on him. Catching face time with the guy—that could be a problem, though. The kinds of clubs where he hangs out leave a lot of people stuck outside the velvet ropes."

"I'll talk to Michelle about using some of her connections to take care of that, too," Liza told him.

They ended the phone call. Liza sat in silence as Michael got onto the freeway.

He shot her a questioning glance. "So we're going to penetrate the secret underworld of hip-hop?"

Liza laughed. "You make it sound like the lair of Fu Manchu."

"I'm not expecting any sinister secret-society types with those wavy daggers," Michael said. "Although we may find some guy from South Central with a beef and a handgun."

"Sounds as if you've been writing too much hard-boiled dialogue," Liza warned him with a laugh. "Keep making cracks like that, and the powers that be will yank your poetic license."

His look became more speculative as they drove along. "I suppose your friend Michelle would be one of those powers."

"She's your friend, too."

Michael shook his head. "She tolerates me—which, I'll admit, is a step up from where I stood before."

Before the whole divorce thing started, Liza realized, but Michael went on.

"What I'm really saying is that the network stretching from her office—all those contacts, connections, and out-and-out spies—that's a spiderweb to make Fu Manchu go green with envy.

"It's kind of funny," Michael continued. "Both Michelle and Don Lowe deal in much the same thing—information and getting it first. Except that most of the time, Michelle is burying it, or trading off it to make something happen."

"While Lowe wants to smear it all over the Internet or TV," Liza said. "Maybe I'm getting old and crotchety, but I've begun to think that there are things people shouldn't have to know."

She paused. "And there's another difference. Lowe generally gets his information with a checkbook. Michelle spent years building her network, making relationships, bartering favors—"

"And maybe just a little terrorism and extortion." Now Michael was the one laughing, although that died away pretty quickly.

"Something *has* changed," he said in a different tone. "Not so long ago, if the tabloids wanted to find out about some celebrity in a hospital, they'd pull a silly stunt like sending a reporter in disguised as a priest. But look at the last election. You had people working in hospitals—people who should know better—leaking the medical records of a candidate."

"It's not just them," Liza said. "People in police departments are leaking information and pictures, too." She shook her head. "Is everybody out there trying to make a quick buck?"

"Maybe it's like crime writing," Michael suggested. "We're just seeing the worst side of society."

"God, I hope so." Liza winced and probed gingerly at her knee. "I think I've been up and around on this too much. Better get home, elevate the knee, and ice it."

"There's something else you may want to discuss with Michelle." A sly laugh crept into Michael's voice.

"What?" Liza asked, bracing herself.

"Should she send you a hot outfit to go clubbing and catch Forty Oz.—or should we send your walker out for detailing? Maybe fire-engine red with a gold flame trim—"

She hit him, but not too hard. After all, they were still on the freeway and had to stay in their lane.

It was early—very early—the next morning that they tried their plan to hook Forty Oz. Liza stifled a yawn in the back of the limousine. She'd tried to nap in the afternoon after hatching this plot with Michelle, but it hadn't worked. Her knee still bothered her, and frankly, she wasn't used to setting off for an evening of partying at two a.m.

She yawned again, stiffening as she saw Michael watching her. "I guess you called it earlier when you said we weren't in Maiden's Bay anymore."

Michael shrugged. "C'mon, Liza, Hollywood is a town where, if you're really working, you start at six in the morning and hit the hay by nine at night." He looked a little sheepish. "Hell, I'm trying not to yawn myself."

He wore a black rough silk shirt and black jeans that, Liza had noticed, fit him very well.

Michelle had sent over some party wear, knowing that Liza's available wardrobe was limited and probably businesslike. Liza had chosen spandex jeans and a red top cut low enough that she wondered how somebody could dance in it. Just moving around with her walker proved unintentionally provocative.

Up in the front of the limo, the driver was speaking back and forth on his cell phone. "They're coming up, and we'll pull in right behind them," he reported.

He sped up a little, took a corner, and then they were on the block that seemed to center on Café Tabú, the latest hot nightspot catering to celebrities and celebrity-watchers. Certainly, Liza saw plenty of the second category—people stretching in a line from midblock to the far corner. They surged against the velvet ropes as Liza's driver brought the car to a stop just behind another limo.

The driver opened the door, and Liza, with Michael's help, worked her way out to a hum of comments and camera flashes.

Although she got out first, the walker slowed Liza down, so she trailed the group of people heading for the club's entrance. The bouncer who had rushed to open the rope for the young woman in the lead now moved to block Liza and Michael from the promised land.

The young woman's back was to this scene, but she turned as if on cue. "They're with me," she said to the big guy in the silk shirt. "My . . . aunt and uncle."

I guess that sounds better than her grandma and grandpa, Liza thought. *And thank God that Delicia Schlissel owed Michelle Markson a favor.*

She stepped past as the bouncer refastened the thin purple velvet line that kept the hoi polloi at bay. Four more heaves of the walker brought Liza to the door of the club, which Michael held open for her. Going through, she found herself surrounded by loud music emerging from a very serious sound system. She knew that from the way bass waves invaded every empty space in her, setting up sympathetic vibrations in her stomach, her lungs, her sinuses . . .

My skull? she wondered as she scanned the crowd on the dance floor. No Forty Oz., though.

Delicia had already seen that, skirting the dancers to head for the VIP lounge. Liza trailed after, letting Delicia deal with more guardians at the gates.

The VIP area was just a roped-off section of tables right off the dance floor. Apparently, the management of Café Tabú didn't want anything really taboo going on. Celebrities were like the floor show—mere mortals could look (or was that gawk?), but they couldn't speak to the favored few.

Liza breezed past an arbiter of exclusivity who seemed to be grinding his teeth.

I guess the walker doesn't add much to the desired ambience around here, she thought.

The celebrity turnout seemed kind of sparse. Was Café Tabú starting to lose its cachet? Maybe it was just too early in the late night for the really hearty partiers. Liza spotted an entourage occupying two tables with Forty Oz. at the center. He was trying to impress a pair of giggling young hardbodies who had competed in one of those best-dancing shows.

Spotting Delicia, the singer's intense face broke into a broad show-biz smile as he rose from his seat with a big hello. Then he fell silent, staring as Liza pulled up beside Delicia.

"Yeah, I know," Liza said. "You feel you ought to recognize me, but you can't remember a name."

That was when the bodyguard rose up from his seat, stepping between Forty Oz. and this apparently deranged stranger. Liza found herself confronting a guy about as wide as a storefront in an imported Italian suit.

She bent around the guy before she was completely

eclipsed. "*D-Kodas*—the makeup department—you were in the chair for special skin tones."

Forty Oz. put his hand on the hulking bodyguard's shoulder. "Right, you were the one who explained the puzzle for the first round we taped. Lena—"

"Liza Kelly," Liza told him. "I need to talk to you about Ritz Tarleton."

The planes of the rapper's face tightened again. "We'll sit over there," he told the bodyguard, pointing to an isolated table. "Keep an eye."

Liza thumped her way over, noticing about halfway that she was timing her walker's movement to the bass beat of the dance music.

This time Michael stayed a couple of paces behind her. Forty Oz. shot him a hostile look when Michael joined them at the table. "And who are you supposed to be?"

"Just the assistant," Michael replied. "Also the husband."

Forty Oz. dismissed him with a look, turning to Liza. "So what's this about Ritz? I know she died in the quake. Is that where you hurt your leg?"

Liza nodded. "What you haven't heard is that the cops have begun to think that Ritz didn't die by accident. They're gonna start digging into everyone who was at Atotori Studios that day."

"Did you know her well?" Michael spoke up.

"We met here and there," Forty Oz. replied. "You know how things are in this town."

"Me, not so much," Michael said. "Liza, on the other hand, knows a lot about Hollywood. Before she went into puzzles, she helped run a publicity agency. Maybe you've heard of her partner? Michelle Markson?"

Forty Oz. didn't say anything, but Liza could read the answer in his expression.

So could Michael. "And you know the information sources she has. According to them, the two of you had a much more . . . extensive relationship. I'm surprised you

don't have a video memento of your time together. She
made at least one other."

Go, Michael, Liza thought. She was so surprised at the
way he dove into this interrogation that she almost missed
the flicker of reaction behind the rapper's poker face. But
Michael didn't just catch it, he ran with it.

"So there is a tape. But why would that worry you? It
should just be another mark on your belt. Unless it makes
you look bad. So what happened? Did she not tell you the
camera was rolling? Did it catch you being sweet to her?
Yeah, that would kill a lot of your hump-'em-and-dump-
'em street cred—"

"All right," the rapper burst out. Four tables away, his
giant guard surged to his feet. Forty Oz. waved him off.

"We hooked up when my first song went gold. I thought
it was just one of the perks. She was older than I was."

And at the time, more famous, Liza thought.

"But Ritz was helpful, showed me the way the whole
celebrity thing worked, and I—" Forty Oz. looked down at
the tabletop. "I ended up having feelings for her. But you
know how they say women are from Venus, men are from
Mars? That one, whoa, she was from Pluto or someplace.
She got real cold on me. How cold, I didn't even realize till
we bumped up on each other at the show. That's when she
told me about the video."

"Why?" Liza asked. "Were you trying to get back together
with her?"

"Not even," the rapper replied. "I barely said hello, and
she started telling me she had something going on and
didn't want me gettin' in the way. And she said she could
make sure I wouldn't be any trouble."

"With that embarrassing video," Michael said. "A real
career killer . . . unless you did something."

"I didn't do a damn thing." Forty Oz. turned to Liza.
"You saw how I did on that puzzle—I couldn't figure out
any damn thing about it. My people told me it would be

easy, but it sure as hell wasn't. Maybe it's just as well they put the shows on whatchacallit—hiatus. Gives me a chance to study some before I try this crap again."

Liza gave him a long, hard look. The celebrity world might be famed for its big egos, but even so, she couldn't see killing someone to gain time for a crash course in sudoku. Of course, Ritz herself had proven willing to engage in a little strong-arm action to make sure she looked good on the show. And the leverage she had on Forty Oz. could be a career killer.

On the other hand, the rapper had been pretty forthcoming after Michael's lucky guess. If he'd killed to keep the video a secret, why would Forty Oz. talk to them about it?

"This 'something' Ritz had going on," Liza said. "Did she give you any idea about what it was?"

"Hell, no," the rapper replied. "She just told me to back off and not get in her way. I didn't even talk to her after that. And then she got that place off on her own with Lolly Popovic." His face went tight again. "Maybe that wasn't such a great idea. Wonder how she felt when it fell in on her."

He fell gloomily silent after that. Liza and Michael exchanged a glance. *I don't think there's anything more he can tell us,* Liza thought.

"I wouldn't want to do too much partying tonight," she warned Forty Oz. "Chances are, in a few hours you'll be getting a visit from Hal Quigley and the celebrity squad."

"We might as well head back to the crib," Forty Oz. said. "Talking with you pretty much killed the mood."

He returned to his entourage, declaring the party over—and causing some people to send fairly dirty looks Liza's way.

Could Forty Oz. have told one of those hangers-on about the video? Liza wondered. *Could they have tried to do something about it—with fatal consequences?*

She looked over the group. Most of the people accompanying Forty Oz. looked interested in spending his money. None of them looked particularly dangerous, except for that brick wall of a bodyguard. And he looked more like a professional than a thug.

We can have Buck Foreman check him out, she decided, *along with the rest of young Forty's known associates.*

She looked over at Michael to see him closing his cell phone with a snap. "Didn't want to disturb you while you were thinking, but I called our driver. I figured that since we couldn't dance, we might as well get out of here."

By the time Liza got up and moving, Forty Oz. and his people were already heading out the door. But no sooner did Liza escape the insistent thump of the music than she found herself facing camera flashes—a lot more than when they went in.

The paparazzi were out in force.

Guess there's not much celebrity news, what with the earthquake and all, Liza thought, grimly thumping along with her walker while photographers converged on Forty Oz., yelling to get his attention.

"Yo, Fawdy!" a young guy with a vaguely familiar face called out, aiming his video camera. "Got any cracks in your walls from the quake?"

Head down, Liza wrestled her walker past him. He glanced away from his viewfinder at her, turned away . . . and then turned back, aiming the camera.

"Haven't I seen you someplace before?" the guy asked.

Liza suddenly recognized the high cheekbones and snub nose of the idiot who'd made the comment about her on *The Lowdown.*

"Maybe," she snarled as she reached her limo, the driver holding the door ready for her.

Liza jerked her head toward Forty Oz. "At least you didn't ask if I was *his* grandmother."

8

Liza yawned, stretched . . . and winced as her knee complained about the sudden movement. She blinked her eyes and looked owlishly around the unfamiliar room.

No, not so unfamiliar; just a room she hadn't been in for a while.

Michael had tried hard to make his office space into a hospitable guest room. His teak computer desk with the swing-out front for a printer had been closed and cleared for the first time in her memory. A bed had been shoehorned into the resulting open space, and someone—maybe Michelle—had attempted to make the place a little cozier, turning the closed-up desk into a combined lamp and cosmetics table with a little mirror with a gilt frame and a marble base, a woven mat, even an antique clock. Nobody could do much about camouflaging the three walls lined with bookcases, though.

No wonder I kept dreaming about being lost in the library, Liza thought.

She'd slept pretty well, although that might be put down

to the late hour when she'd gotten home and the painkiller she'd popped before going to bed.

Liza gingerly worked herself to the foot of the bed and slipped into the robe she'd left there. There wasn't a hell of a lot of space to maneuver the walker, but she made it to the door and then to the bathroom.

She emerged to find Michael already up, clad in an old T-shirt pulled over a pair of sweats. "Morning," he said. "Feel like some breakfast?"

Liza took a deep breath, savoring the scent of coffee already on the drip. "Mmmmmm. Coffee. Good."

Michael nodded. "Yes, coffee good. Breakfast better. Want some?"

"Want lots," Liza replied with a grin, getting her walker into motion.

When they got installed in the kitchen, they had a very cheerful breakfast of pancakes, eggs, orange juice, and coffee.

"You pulled out all the stops," Liza said, chasing a smear of maple syrup on her plate with her last forkful of pancake.

"It must have done good work," Michael replied. "You're speaking in full sentences again."

Laughing, Liza settled back in her chair with a cup of coffee. Then the phone rang.

As Michael answered, his smile faded away. "Yes, she is here." He stepped over to hand Liza the handset.

Liza raised it to her ear. "This is Liza Kelly."

"Could you hold, please, for Mr. Tarleton?"

Well, now I can understand Michael's expression, Liza thought in the brief interval before another voice came on—a much shorter interval than usual for executive suite politicos.

"Ms. Kelly, I'm sorry to impose on you."

The last time Liza had heard that voice, Fritz Tarleton

had confidently expected to push on with a hunt for a dead man's treasure. The tourism tycoon sounded a lot more tentative now.

"You certainly tracked me down," Liza told him. They had been rivals that last time around, and Michelle had played pretty rough to make him back off.

"I—I'd like to meet with you, if possible. About what happened—" His voice broke. "About what happened to Ritz."

Liza looked at the phone. The usually imperious Mr. Tarleton was almost begging her.

"Perhaps an hour—" She glanced down at her robe. "Or maybe an hour and a half?"

She was about to ask where his office was, but he surprised her, saying, "I'll be out there in an hour and a half, then."

After a shower and a change of clothes, Liza found herself in the recliner, her hurt knee elevated—and her walker out of reach.

Maybe that's just as well, she ruefully told herself. In normal circumstances, she'd be creating a rut in the rug pacing back and forth in anticipation of Fritz Tarleton's arrival. Unfortunately, neither her walker nor her knee was exactly up to that job right now.

Michael had stationed himself by the living room window, peeking out at the street from behind the curtain.

"There's a limousine pulling into the driveway," he finally reported. "That should interest the neighbors—two limos in as many days."

He rushed over to the front door and had it open probably before Tarleton's chauffeur had done the same job on the limo.

Fritz Tarleton looked out of place in the comfortable but slightly shabby living room.

The fact was, the price of his haircut could probably

finance a replacement for the sofa. The money that went into his suit could probably renovate the whole living room—and get a start on the kitchen, too.

The man inside the expensive clothing had that George Clooney/John Forsythe look, Central Casting's vision of the high-powered business executive.

Liza remembered that from her previous run-in with Tarleton. He acted as if his money and power could allow him to get his way against anyone. It had taken Michelle Markson and an embarrassing sex video Ritz had recorded of herself to get Fritz Tarleton to back down.

Now, however, the tourism tycoon seemed somehow . . . shrunken.

Was that a result of the financial meltdown, or was it the loss of his daughter?

Tarleton seemed to be reading her mind. "I'm sorry we got off on the wrong foot when we first met," he said. "I was so hypnotized by the idea of getting that painting that I acted like a prize jerk."

He shook his head. "Guess I learned a little late about what's really important. Like my little girl."

Tarleton looked down at her, his expression admitting the irony of his words, but his eyes showing a pain that broke Liza's heart. "She was a little girl once, you know. As for what she grew up to be—"

He broke off. "Now I'm hearing rumors that her death may not be the accident we thought at first. My sources may not be as extensive as your partner's, but they're good enough." Tarleton paused. "They also tell me you're asking some questions about Ritz."

"It's not—I haven't—" Liza floundered for a minute, trying to explain what she was doing and realizing that she didn't really have a clear idea of that herself. She took a deep breath. "I don't want to intrude on something that's obviously painful for you. There were just some questions about what Ritz had on her mind before the earthquake."

Fritz Tarleton sank into a chair off to the side of the sofa, giving her a long look. "You think I'm here to tell you to stay out of this, to forget about Ritz." He gave her a very definite headshake. "I came to offer any help I can with an investigation. I've already told my head of security, Jim McShane, to give you any information he can, nothing held back."

"I'm not sure what I'm investigating," Liza said, embarrassed. "And I certainly can't make any promises—"

"I'm only too aware of that." Tarleton's regular features tightened as he spoke. "But you've managed to get to the bottom of some pretty odd cases—cases the police might not have solved. And I'm not trying to tell you what to do—only that there are resources available if you need them."

Liza stewed for a few seconds more, unwilling to commit herself. She looked over at Michael, who stood behind Tarleton. He shrugged and held out empty hands, as unsure about what to say as she was.

"I don't know what the police are looking into, and I'm not sure this really has any connection to what happened," Liza told the tour baron. "But I've heard from several people that Ritz had something going, and it involved the celebrity competition on *D-Kodas*. Do you have any idea what that might be?"

Fritz Tarleton slowly shook his head. "I don't know what exactly she might have been up to. But I guess I shouldn't be too surprised, after my last conversation with her."

Michael leaned forward. "What was that?"

Tarleton sighed. "It was the end of a conversation extending over several months, about . . . what Ritz was supposed to do when she grew up."

He looked the picture of a baffled father. "When she turned twenty-five, I told Ritz she had to develop some talent other than picking up checks. She wanted me to put up the money to option a script and produce a movie for her. I told her it was high time that she developed some interest in the family business. She spent about a month traveling around, touching base with some of the key people in our operation."

His lips puckered, as if he'd just taken a healthy swallow of vinegar masquerading as fine wine. "She told me it was boring."

Liza had nothing to say to that. For a man who had devoted himself to upgrading his father's package tour business, making the connections to create a deluxe travel operation, Ritz's comment couldn't have gone down well.

"So what did you do?" Michael asked.

"I pointed out that with her background, she could make an excellent ambassador for the business." Even the memory of the conversation made Tarleton's temper flare. "All she had to do was apply herself. Instead, she came to me with some harebrained idea about underwriting the pilot for a sitcom she could star in."

Anger and anguish warred on Tarleton's face. "I told her it was time she started living in reality—that from here on, the bank was closed." He shot them a pleading look. "She had a separate trust fund from her grandmother—I thought she could live on that while she thought about her options. How was I to know she'd run through that money already?"

Liza figured it was her turn to ask a question. "So what did Ritz do?"

"Her mother told me that she tried to get onto one of those reality shows. There was *Celebrity Undercover*, where they were supposed to go out and take different jobs week after week, with the one fooling the most people winning. Then she tried for Trump's show. But her competition was either more famous or younger. Ritz thought she had a shot at becoming a regular on one of those celebrity prank shows. From the way she could always talk people into doing things, she thought she'd be a natural for that. But the show fell through. I think she tried for one of those celebrity gossip shows, and then there was the dancing show."

"We heard how that turned out," Liza said. "It must have been a bitter pill for her to swallow when all she could get was Celebrity Week on *D-Kodas*." Ritz had never been a brightly shining star. But lately even that had been fading. Now it turned out she wasn't just being hit in the ego, but in the wallet, too.

"But don't you see?" Exasperation burst through Fritz Tarleton's pain. "Being the Tarleton Tours ambassador would have been all about celebrity—publicity, going to the most glamorous places on Earth . . ."

Except that to the people in Ritz's circle, the ones she wanted to impress, it would seem more like being a glorified tour guide, or the hostess in a restaurant . . . or even the chauffeur for your limo, Liza thought. But Fritz Tarleton couldn't see that, just as he didn't realize that while his clients might be rich and famous, they just considered him a travel agent.

Tarleton slumped in his chair. "Was that such a bad thing?" he asked, his voice plaintive.

"I wouldn't think so," Liza carefully replied. "But I guess it wasn't what Ritz wanted."

Fritz Tarleton sat silent for a moment and then slowly got up. "I hope you can figure out some way to go at this." His voice was heavy as he spoke. He knew he was missing something in this situation, but Liza found herself hoping he wouldn't figure out how Ritz must have felt.

"Remember, if there's anything you need . . ." Tarleton fumbled in the inside pocket of his suit jacket, coming out with two Tarleton Tours business cards. One had his name and direct office line. The other was for Jim McShane, the security director.

"Uh—thanks." Liza sounded as awkward as she felt, pushing herself up on the arm of the couch, balancing on her good leg. "I guess we'll have to wait and see if there are any developments."

They shook hands and she watched him go out to his limo.

Michael came back from closing the door. "So what do you think?" he said briskly. "Should we follow along the path of Ritz's ambassadorial tour? With luck, our investigation could take us to Hawaii or Acapulco."

"I think that would be taking advantage of a very distraught man." Liza plumped down onto the couch and let out a little yelp of pain. *Still playing too rough for that knee,* she told herself.

Aloud, she said, "We got a bit more motive for whatever scam Ritz was pulling, but no specifics about what she was up to."

"We still have a few of the celebrity contestants left to talk to," Michael suggested. "Maybe Ritz said something to them. Claudio Day is off in Denver for an exhibition game, and I guess Samantha Pang is back teaching—where was that? San Francisco, I think."

Liza gave him a look. "Before you start suggesting a weekend at the Sir Francis Drake Hotel to go and interview her, I've got to say that this knee isn't up for an extended road trip."

She thought for a moment. "Wish Dudek could probably rustle up a phone number for Sam Pang. And maybe Buck could do the same for Claudio Day."

As things turned out, Michelle Markson got the contact number for Claudio Day, through the football player's sports agent. That agent had also promised to call Day and give him the heads-up, but the quarterback sounded surprised and a little hazy to hear from her.

First rule of Hollywood, Liza thought sourly. *Never trust anything an agent tells you.*

"Yes, Liza Kelly," she repeated for the third time. "Arlie

Macomber gave me this number. We met on the set of *D-Kodas*." Liza fought to keep her sigh from becoming audible. "No, not Arlie and me; *you* and me. I explained the rules for the first puzzle."

"Y'know," Claudio said, "I don't think that was as clear as it could have been."

"I'm sorry you feel that way," Liza told him. *Maybe you should have read through the explanation and practice puzzles in your briefing book,* she added in her brain.

"Arlie said it would be easy—show people what I looked like in front of the cameras, maybe get a little TV or movie work, you know what I'm sayin'?"

People have been sayin' that or some variation of it for about a hundred years now, Liza thought. Instead she said, semi-truthfully, "I was talking to Ritz Tarleton's father today. He's working on the eulogy and trying to get together some recent remembrances from—"

"Yeah, I heard about her. That's messed up," Claudio interrupted.

Liza gritted her teeth. "So I was wondering if the people who had been with her during her last appearance might have something to say."

"Like me?" Claudio sounded really surprised now. "I don't think she said three words to me on the set that day."

"Had you met her before the day you taped?" Liza pressed on.

"No." Claudio paused for a second. "Well, yes. I bumped into her a month or so ago at a fund-raiser. Sports scholarships for poor kids. Frankly, I was a little surprised. It didn't seem like the kind of thing where you'd see Ritz Tarleton turning up. So we talked, and it was kind of funny—like she was checking me out."

He gave a quick, nervous laugh. "Not that I was interested or anything. I've got a wife—"

And I'm sure she'd be glad to hear all about this, Liza thought.

"And, you know, Ritz has—had—a bit of a rep," the football player went on. "Anyway, we talked for maybe five minutes, and that was that. Next time I saw her was at the show, and then she was like, 'Hi, howyadoin'.'" He paused again, a bit put out. "She didn't even wish me good luck or anything."

Breathing a silent sigh of relief that Claudio didn't have anything to add to her fictitious eulogy, Liza thanked the quarterback and disconnected the call.

"So?" Michael asked. "Was there any connection?"

"There was, but not the way Claudio thought," Liza replied slowly. "He thought she was checking him out."

Michael's eyebrows rose. "À la Forty Oz.?"

Liza nodded. "Although Claudio was quick to remind me that he had a wife. But I don't think that's what Ritz was checking out. Claudio's not the sharpest tool in the workshop. I think that once Ritz was sure he wouldn't be any competition for her on *D-Kodas*, she didn't even bother with him."

She sat silent for a moment, gently rubbing her hurt knee and frowning. "One other thing. Ritz arranged to bump into Claudio a month before the taping."

Michael looked confused.

"Back then, Sukey Tupp was still the official contestant. Whatever Ritz was doing, she was planning it well in advance."

Liza caught Samantha Pang at home early in the evening. The mathematician didn't buy into Liza's eulogy story at all.

"I know we're not supposed to speak ill of the dead." Sam Pang's voice trembled a little. "But I can't say I'm sorry about what happened to Ritz Tarleton. Okay, maybe having a house fall on her was a bit much—but then, she acted like a wicked witch to me."

Liza didn't even get a chance to ask a question—Sam

just sucked in a breath and went on. "I can't believe how stupid I was, falling for her nice act. It's bad enough she made me up like a clown; she made a fool of me, too. But that's not the worst of it—she took pictures, too."

Liza thought back to the scene in the makeup department. Yes, she'd heard a click behind her, and when she turned around, Ritz had pocketed something.

A cell phone camera, Liza thought.

"That night, she sent me a picture—I looked like Bozette!" Sam almost wailed. "I think she sent me a dumb sudoku, too—the thing didn't even work. Then the next morning, she caught me alone and said, 'I'll make it clear—either you dial down your game today, or tomorrow your picture will be the lead story on *The Lowdown*.'"

"But you got the first of the magic squares in the first puzzle," Liza said.

"I was so angry, at first I thought, 'The hell with it,'" Samantha said. "But every time I looked at the puzzle, that picture kept coming up in front of me. I got scared. She could have made me a laughingstock, not just to people watching television, but to my students and, worse, my academic peers. Oh, nobody would say anything out loud, but would a clown get tenure, promotions? This could have wrecked my whole career."

Sam Pang gulped for air. "So I *did* dial it back, and Ritz won the game. If that earthquake hadn't hit . . . What the hell did she *want*?"

"I'm wondering if we'll ever know," Liza said soberly.

"I just want to forget it." Sam's voice came tightly over the line. "But I keep thinking that picture of me is still out there somewhere. Do you think if I asked the police, they might erase it from her phone?"

I think if you asked the wrong cop, you might wind up on The Lowdown *anyway,* Liza thought.

"Maybe you'd want to wait until Ritz's personal effects

come back to her father," Liza advised. "Mr. Tarleton is a reasonable man. If you want, I'll talk to him."

"Thank you," Sam said. "I'll take any help I can get. This is killing me, Ms. Kelly."

They ended the phone call, and Liza told Michael about the photograph.

"So we have one warning and two attempts at blackmail."

"And one contestant too dumb to bother with," Liza finished for him.

"Or maybe not so dumb," Michael argued. "Chard Switzer, Forty Oz., and Sam Pang were pretty up-front about Ritz twisting their arms, admitting to motives to murder her."

"The cops aren't publicly talking about murder yet," Liza pointed out.

Michael nodded. "So they don't see any problem with coming clean about it. The only one who'd deny having any motive would be someone who knows a murder was committed—because he was the murderer."

Liza stared at him. "So, by that logic, you're saying that Claudio Day . . ."

"He plays pro football, where even the quarterbacks are big, strong guys." Michael made a violent pushing motion. "He'd have the muscle to send Ritz flying. That's means. I guess we'll have to look into opportunity while Buck digs into motive."

Michael sat down beside Liza on the couch, reaching for the TV remote. "That seems to be all we can do right now. *The Lowdown* is coming on now. Let's see if Sam Pang's picture turns up on this edition."

The lead story didn't feature Sam. Instead, Liza saw Forty Oz. and his entourage coming out of Café Tabú—and then her own angry face telling the cameraman that she wasn't the rapper's grandmother.

The image froze, and Don Lowe appeared with his signature clipboard. "She may not be a household name, but

Liza Kelly has a certain amount of celebrity for writing about puzzles—and solving murders."

His face filled the screen as he looked straight into the camera. "What a coincidence that she seems to be following one of the last people who saw Ritz Tarleton alive—especially since we hear that LAPD investigators are now treating her death as a murder."

9

The next five minutes of *The Lowdown* presented a video eulogy for Ritz Tarleton. Liza watched bikini clips from Ritz's beach-bunny days doing her father's travel show. Then came a series of glamour scenes of Ritz attending Hollywood premieres with A-list types.

There were no mug shots, however—Don Lowe and company had decided to gloss over her follies—although they did show Ritz smirking in the background as one of her friends did a reenactment of the Marilyn Monroe subway-grating pose—this time without any underwear.

Liza just sat through the whole sequence in shock until Michael handed her the phone—she hadn't even realized it was ringing.

"Well, I suppose I should be glad you didn't give that paparazzo the finger," Michelle Markson told her crisply. "Though why I should be repeating to you of all people the basic rule about keeping a low profile while cameras are around—"

She broke off, abruptly changing gears. "Usually I'd say any publicity is good publicity. I'm not sure, though, if it's helpful for a discreet investigation to be plastered across the airwaves on a celebrity gossip show."

"It won't please the people I've spoken with," Liza admitted. "Nor will it please the cops to have their investigation leaked onto national syndication."

"Not to mention the fact that you're competing with them." Michelle's voice was interrupted by a call-waiting beep. "I'll get off, trusting my point has been made. If that interruption turns out to be a press inquiry, perhaps you'd be better off referring them to me."

"I'm not answering it," Liza assured her partner. But as soon as she hung up the receiver, the phone began to ring.

A second later, another ringtone chimed in from the cell phone in Liza's bag. Then Michael's cell began to bleat.

"What are we going to do?" Liza asked.

"Switch them all to silent mode and let voice mail deal with the idiots." Michael was already fiddling with his cell phone's keypad. Then he turned off the ringer on the landline, dug out Liza's phone for her to reset, rejoined her on the couch, and picked up the remote. "In the meantime, let's see if we can find a nice, safe, old sitcom we can watch instead of the news."

Liza ignored the phone through the evening and the early morning by immersing herself in sudoku, manually creating new puzzles. After all, her cushion—the stockpile of columns already in the hands of her editor—wouldn't last forever.

She had just finished a fairly tough sudoku when their privacy bubble was popped by an official house call from Detective Hal Quigley.

At least there aren't any film crews lurking outside to catch this, Liza consoled herself as she stacked the puzzles beside her on the sofa.

Quigley didn't even bother to maintain a cop's usual

	6						1	
8			3		9			4
4				5				9
	1			8			6	
2				7				3
3			2		4			7
	5						8	

impassive expression as he sat down beside Liza. He
brushed a finger over her sudoku efforts, his anchormanly
features twisted in a frown.

"It's sudoku," she said, gathering up the pages. "It's my
business."

"Then I wish you'd mind your own instead of pushing
your nose into mine," he told her gruffly. "Do I have to
remind you that impeding a police investigation is a crime?"

"I'm not impeding anything," Liza replied. "Before she
died, Ritz Tarleton did hurtful things to several people—
including friends of mine. I was just trying to find out why—"

"And considering your experience with the other murder
cases you've interfered in, you didn't think Ms. Tarleton's
actions might, just possibly, contribute to a motive for her
death?"

Liza phrased her answer carefully. She wasn't supposed
to know for sure that Quigley and his squad were treating

Ritz's death as a murder. But she couldn't be sure that Quigley hadn't already questioned Buck Foreman. "The people I spoke with seemed pretty forthcoming about their relationships with Ritz. I had no expectation that they'd say anything different to you."

Quigley's lips made a tight line as he looked at her. "So what, exactly, did they say?"

Liza recounted the stories that Chard, Forty Oz., Samantha Pang, and Claudio Day had told her. When she finished, she asked, "Did they say anything different to you?"

"Not in the end," Quigley conceded. "Ms. Pang, for one, was more evasive when I questioned her."

"Several of them faced severe embarrassment because of Ritz," Liza offered.

"That's an interesting way to characterize attempted extortion," Quigley said bluntly. He leaned forward, his faded blue eyes concentrating on Liza's face. "And one of the people I spoke with can't even account for her whereabouts at the time of the fatal attack."

Please let it be Darrie Brunswick, Liza silently prayed.

"Who might that be?" Michael asked, his voice as tight as Liza's insides felt.

Quigley looked over at him. "That's right—you're a friend of Rikki Popovic's. And the two of you had dinner the other evening with her and her daughter, Lolly."

Liza went with the honest answer to his unasked question. "She asked me for some career advice."

"Well, now she may be looking for some legal advice." Quigley's eyebrows rose as he looked back and forth between Michael and Liza. "You didn't know about that? How odd. Asking all those questions of virtual strangers—I wonder why you didn't ask your friends about Ritz Tarleton."

He rose to his feet. "Since that idiot on TV leaked the information that we're investigating a murder, I don't suppose it will be long before news of a person of interest comes out." He shook his head in polite disbelief. "Lolly Popovic claims she doesn't know what happened during the earthquake. If you believe her, she has amnesia."

Quigley walked out before either Liza or Michael got over their shock. When the door swung shut, Michael finally moved to the window. "He's gone," he reported, "not hanging around to eavesdrop."

He turned from the window, standing silent for a moment. Liza recognized the expression—the writer was trying to find the words. "I appreciate that you respected my friendship with Rikki—that you didn't start right in asking questions about Lolly."

Liza shrugged. "I'd met her already, and she didn't have much to say about Ritz." She looked down at the rug. "To tell the truth, when all this nonsense started, I didn't *want* to talk to Lolly. I figured she would be the one the cops would be all over. After all, she was the one who left the soundstage with Ritz—supposedly on the way to the Boots Bungalow."

Her eyes met Michael's. "And when you didn't suggest going after Lolly, I figured I'd go along, seeing whether the other people involved with Ritz might explain what the hell she was doing."

His shoulders hunched a little. "But we haven't gotten any answers." Michael paused for a second. "What do you think about this amnesia business?"

"You did a bit of research about that for some scripts, didn't you?" Liza asked.

Michael frowned in thought. "Lolly took a head injury—that could really mess up a person's memories, not just after, but even before she got hurt."

"So she honestly might not recall any events that happened around the earthquake." Now it was Liza's turn to pause. "The problem is, that sounds like the kind of script you might write."

"The kind of script that wouldn't get accepted because

it strains the audience's willing suspension of disbelief,"
Michael glumly agreed. "We've got to talk with Lolly—
although I don't know how we can make that happen after
Quigley warned us off."

"Well, wait a second," Liza said. "He warned us against
impeding his investigation. He didn't particularly forbid us
to talk with Lolly."

Michael gave her a long, silent look. "I think you've
been spending too much time hanging around Alvin Hunzinger, lawyer to the stars," he finally said. "That's slicing
the baloney mighty fine."

"Frankly, I was sort of wishing we had Alvin around
when Quigley was here. For a while I think he was debating whether he wanted to arrest me, you, or both of us."

Usually, Michael would laugh at a line like that. This
time, though, he merely nodded. "Let's just hope he didn't
decide to leave us at large in the hopes we can get Lolly to
implicate herself."

Getting hold of the Popovics turned into a much more difficult job than either Michael or Liza expected. They ran
through all the numbers they had collected from Rikki
and Lolly at dinner—could it really have been only five
evenings before?

Michael put down the phone with a frustrated thump.
"The curse of voice mail strikes again," he announced.
"And that was our last number for them."

"I guess we shouldn't be surprised," Liza said. "We did
the same thing after my face appeared on *The Lowdown*."

"Well, yeah," Michael admitted. "But I didn't have to
get in touch with you then. Or if I did, I knew you couldn't
be more than ten feet away from the couch."

He ducked as Liza sent one of the decorative cushions
flying at his head.

"Maybe you could give Buck a call and see if he'll check

on them," Liza suggested. She waited until Michael was bending to get the phone again, and then clobbered him with the couch's other pillow.

"Let that be a warning to you," she told him. "I may be part crippled, but I'm still not to be messed with."

Buck's report, which Michael put on the speakerphone, was not encouraging. "They've apparently left their place in Malibu." Buck's usually deep voice sounded even more ominous with the speaker's rain-barrel effect. "I guess they're officially in seclusion."

"And Rikki's been kicking around Hollywood for a good twenty-five years." Michael slumped sideways in the armchair. "I'm betting she knows some really secluded places for seclusion."

He suddenly sat up straight again. "Unless . . . I can think of one place they'll probably have to be fairly soon. The doctor who took care of her at that hospital in Bel Air will want Lolly back to have her head examined."

Liza rolled her eyes. "She won't be the only one if we have to go and stake the place out."

Buck managed to make their job easier, finding out when Lolly's appointment was. So Liza and Michael didn't have to put hours into staking out the hospital entrance. Even so, they almost missed their quarry.

Liza gazed around in boredom as a woman with her arm in a sling came up to the door. The woman opened it, looked around, and then made a beckoning gesture.

Michael suddenly jerked upright in his seat. "That's Rikki Popovic."

It took Liza a moment, but she finally managed to look through the makeup and see the actress underneath. Rikki had done a masterful job of toning down her natural beauty. She'd done something to make her hair more drab, hollowed out her cheeks, and added dark rings around her

eyes—and the baggy clothes she wore not only camou-
flaged her figure, but actually made her look fat and dumpy.

Now she stood with her back holding open the hospital door, looking toward a cab parked at the curb where
another figure emerged.

Lolly Popovic had received a similar makeover job to
dial back her natural beauty. She wore an oversized baseball
cap to hide the bandages on her head while oversized clothing muffled her figure. As she covered the distance across
the sidewalk, her eyes kept moving nervously around.

Lolly was right to be nervous. When Lolly was halfway
to the entrance, the passenger door on a parked SUV swung
open and a familiar figure piled out, videocam at the ready.

"Hey, Lolly, are you afraid the police are actually going
to arrest you?" The reporter from *The Lowdown* flung back
his head to shake the long, lank hair out of his eyes. His
big blue eyes had a more serious glint than usual, and his
high cheekbones had flushed pink—with excitement? Or
was that anger?

Could he have been drinking? Liza wondered as she
heaved herself out of Michael's Honda.

From the machine-gun volley of questions coming out
of the guy's mouth, he had to be high on something.

"You know they think you did it, don't you, Lolly? Did
you do it? *Did* you? Why? Why would you kill Ritz?" His
voice cracked on his last demand—not that he got an answer.

Lolly stood frozen in the middle of the sidewalk, pale
and trembling, her mouth hanging open in shock.

That's bad, Liza thought, hauling herself up on her
walker. *It makes her look guilty.*

Michael had already barreled out from behind the steer-
ing wheel, moving to interpose himself between Lolly and
her tormentor.

But Rikki Popovic was even quicker.

Charging like a lioness defending her cub, she rammed
into the guy from *The Lowdown.*

Wow, she must have some muscles under all those curves,
Liza thought.

The video paparazzo almost executed a somersault in
midair before he crashed down on the curbside, nearly at
Liza's feet.

Before he could get up, Liza positioned her walker over
his chest, blocking any possible shot. She rested her full
weight on the frame as he rattled against it.

"Get out of my way! Move this thing!" the reporter angrily
demanded.

Liza moved it, all right, bringing one of the legs thumping down in a poke where she thought it would do him the
most good—or was that harm?

The paparazzo let out a yelp that turned into a yell.
"Goddammit, lady, I might want to have kids someday, you
know!" He let go of his camera, both hands going to cup
himself as he curled up in pain.

Gritting her teeth against the complaints from her
injured knee, Liza brought her walker up and over the
reporter, smacking one of the legs against his video camera
and sending it skittering into a nearby storm drain.

The reporter's language got downright sulfurous as
he struggled upright—well, not exactly upright. He stood
hunched over, still clutching his injured parts. When he
realized that Lolly and Rikki had escaped—and where his
camera had gone—he grew even louder and more inventive.

Liza looked at him. "Young man," she said in her most
rebuking tone, "don't you realize this is a hospital zone?
You're supposed to keep quiet."

Michael appeared beside her, helping her back into the
Honda. They escaped as the video paparazzo shouted impo-
tently behind them.

"Mission accomplished?" Liza asked from the backseat, rubbing her knee.

*It's never going to get better if I keep jumping around
on it,* she thought ruefully.

"I gave Rikki the number for that throwaway cell phone we picked up on the way over here," Michael reported as he steered them toward the freeway. "Although I had a moment or two of doubt and fear that she was going to tear my head off before she recognized me."

They stopped for a red light, and he shot her a wry look. "From what I saw you doing to that *Lowdown* guy, you're having altogether too much fun with that walker."

Liza shot him a smile. "It's just like you said in that Sherlock Holmes script you tried to sell—'Watson, any item can become a deadly weapon.'"

"That was 'infernal device,'" Michael corrected her. Then after a second he admitted, "Although 'deadly weapon' probably sounds better."

"I wonder," Liza said in a distracted voice.

"About what?" Michael asked with a little annoyance. "I just agreed that you had the better line."

"What?" Liza shook her head. "Sorry; I jumped to something completely different. I was wondering about that video paparazzo."

"You mean, will he be able to have children after that poke you gave him?" Michael asked with a grin. "In spite of all his yelling, I think the answer is 'yes.'"

Liza didn't laugh at that, though. "Did you get a look at the guy's face while he was interviewing Lolly?"

"If you could call that an interview," Michael said. "It wasn't just an ambush. That was more like an attack."

"The questions got a little much, even for *The Lowdown*." Liza frowned. "In fact, when he talked about Ritz, it sounded more personal than professional."

She started scrabbling around for her cell phone. "I'm going to call Buck. Maybe we have another person with a connection to Ritz."

10

Before she even began punching in the number, Liza heard the bleating of a cell phone. "That's not mine," she said.

"Not mine, either," Michael told her. "I didn't choose that ringtone."

"It's the throwaway!"

Liza rummaged around on the backseat to find the bag from the cell phone store. She managed to find their undercover phone and hit the appropriate button before the ringing stopped.

"Michael?" The reception was so rough, static made Rikki Popovic's voice sound gravelly.

Note to self, Liza thought. *If we ever have to do this again, spring for the expensive coverage plan.*

"This is Liza," she said into the phone. "Are you and Lolly okay?"

"Yes, after we got away from that maniac," Rikki said. "Michael said you wanted to meet with us. Can you do it now?"

"Sure," Liza replied. "The only question is, where?"

They quickly decided on a meeting place.

Michael continued driving down Beverly Glen to Santa Monica Boulevard, heading southwest toward the Pacific Ocean. A few blocks short of the beach, he made a quick left, then a right, and he rolled to a stop in the parking area for the Santa Monica Pier.

Liza got out her walker and set off along with Michael through the arched entranceway, past the amusement park, and onto the pier.

"Funny how we'd go all the way down to Balboa when we had an amusement pier so close to home," Michael said, looking at the carousel, the roller coaster, and the Ferris wheel. "They even put up a new Ferris wheel—solar power."

"Great if you're determined to go green." Liza halted over her walker. "Our Ferris wheel is different." She gave him a lopsided grin. "It's powered with golden memories."

He smiled back. "Of course, there is that."

Liza peered through the railing edging the pier. "Let's go farther," she said. "The tide is out. Kind of ridiculous to stand on a pier if all you have under you is beach."

With Michael at her side, she humped along a bit farther until the surf was sloshing against the pier pilings below. Liza stopped next to the railing to look down.

When she looked up, she saw Rikki and Lolly Popovic coming to join them.

Liza glanced around, but nobody on the pier seemed to be paying any attention to the pair of dumpy tourists meeting up with their gimpy friend.

Lolly grabbed Liza's hand. "Thank you for holding that man down. After he started yelling those crazy things at me, I couldn't even move."

"I didn't do all that much." Liza tried to downplay the whole thing.

"You hit him where it counted and got rid of his camera," Rikki cut in. "Thank God for that. This has been enough of a nightmare without people streaming crazy footage like that on the net."

"Yeah, we had a visit from Detective Quigley," Michael said. "He didn't strike me as much like a fun guy."

"That one!" Rikki's voice dripped venom. "From the moment he talked with my daughter, it was clear he wasn't after information. He wanted a suspect, the more famous, the better."

"And I couldn't tell him anything." Lolly leaned against the pier's steel railing as if it were the only thing holding her up.

"Do you remember hitting your head?" Michael asked, nodding toward the bandages hidden under Lolly's baseball cap.

She shook her head. "I recall taping the first game, and Ritz picking me. That was a surprise. Then they called a break, and we were going . . . somewhere." Her eyes looked lost and afraid. "Next thing I knew, I was in the hospital. They'd just stitched up my scalp."

Her hand tentatively went to the side of her head. "A nurse at the hospital said that studio guards found me at the New York standing set."

Liza nodded. Certain areas of the studio grounds had been built up as different locations—the Wild West, or small-town America, a few blocks of Paris, and a section that could double as downtown New York, or Chicago, or any other big-city locale.

"From the looks of you, is much of that set standing anymore?" Liza tried to joke.

Rikki took her seriously. "The brick front on one of the buildings peeled off—a falling piece clipped Lolly. If she'd been just a step or two over—"

Lolly shuddered. "I'd be dead, too."

Michael's face got an intent look as he glanced between mother and daughter. "Do they know when the building fell?"

Sure, Liza thought. *If those bricks fell during the first tremor, that would place Lolly away from Ritz—give her an alibi.*

Rikki saw where he was going and shook her head. "Nothing was shooting in the area, so no one was there. Nobody knows."

Liza frowned, trying to remember her studio geography. The Boots Bungalow was part of the small-town America area—and wasn't all that far from the fake big-city downtown.

If Lolly ran that way after pushing Ritz into the collapsing bungalow during the first tremor, she could have reached the city set just in time to get conked on the head by the second quake. Liza tried to keep her face neutral as she considered that scenario.

She looked into Lolly's eyes, seeing the confusion and terror there.

I've spent years in show business, with more actors than I can count trying to blow smoke up my butt, she thought. *If Lolly is faking this . . .*

Well, Lolly had been portraying different roles since early childhood. It would take supreme acting ability to play the part of an innocent.

Liza looked at the young woman again. She seemed genuinely mystified. That and the fear flickering in the backs of Lolly's eyes convinced Liza that the amnesia story was for real.

If that were so, then not even Lolly knew what happened in the Boots Bungalow. That meant it was possible that she had indeed killed Ritz—for a reason she now couldn't remember.

Okay, then. The job was to find out what Lolly did remember, and see how it fit with what Liza and Michael had found out so far.

Liza decided to try to circle in slowly for what she needed. "Ritz didn't try to make herself very popular on the set. In fact, she seemed determined to go in pretty much the opposite direction."

Lolly nodded. "She got into a fight with Darrie Brunswick." She looked at her mother. "Didn't you tell me that?"

"You were there," Liza said gently. "Darrie got so worked up, the producer decided to call an early lunch to give her some time to try and calm down."

Rikki pounced on the possibility. "So there's one person that Quigley man should be looking at."

"One of many." Liza chose her words carefully, not wanting to give away any of the secrets people had entrusted her with. "Ritz had information that could have embarrassed Forty Oz. and Samantha Pang, and let them know about that. She also put some personal pressure on Chard Switzer. All of them said she was up to something, but none of them knew exactly what that might be."

She took a deep breath. "So I have to ask you, Lolly. How was Ritz with you? Did she say anything?"

Lolly could only shake her head helplessly. "She was . . . I don't know, kind of weird. When they heard I'd be on the show with her, friends warned me that Ritz had a bizarre sense of humor—like the way she got Chard Switzer to change his name."

"He told us about that," Michael said.

"But she never did anything and barely said anything to me." Lolly gave an uncomfortable shrug. "But every once in a while, I'd catch her looking at me, and she'd have this really creepy smile."

"You never told me about that." Rikki Popovic's voice was sharp.

"Mom, it's like I said. She never did anything. When we talked she was all business, concentrating on the show. She even gave me some puzzles to practice on."

Lolly glanced over at Liza. "She said she'd taken a class with you and could even make up her own sudoku."

Looks as if Ritz didn't mention where *she took the class,*

Liza thought. "I wouldn't say she was my smartest student," she said.

"I guess not," Lolly agreed. "When I tried to work out one of them, I couldn't get anywhere. It was all messed up."

Liza found herself intrigued. "Do you still have them?"

Lolly nodded. "Sure. We had the same Solv-a-Doku app on our phones."

"Oh." Liza had helped to work on the original Solv-a-Doku program, but she hadn't heard about this latest development. "I don't think my phone—"

"I've got it on mine," Michael said. He gave Lolly his number. She dug out her cell phone and started transferring the puzzles.

Rikki gave them both a skeptical look. "You think those puzzles mean something?"

From the look on her face, she thought they were all wasting valuable time.

"I just wanted to see how Ritz was using what I taught her," Liza answered. "Who knows? Maybe there's even a column in it."

"That's right." Rikki's voice got a bit colder. "You're a journalist now." The way she said it, "journalist" and "enemy" were about the same thing in her dictionary.

Liza sighed. She'd seen this reaction before. "I write about sudoku," she told Rikki. "There's very little breaking news in that field."

But apparently even the thought of journalists made Rikki nervous. "We've been staying at a motel not too far from here," she said. "Maybe we should be moving."

Lolly laughed. "Mom makes sure we have our bags packed whenever we leave the room."

"Not such a bad idea." *If you're on the run,* Liza added silently. *Michael's right. Rikki knows a lot about the going-into-seclusion thing.*

"Would you mind giving us a lift?" Lolly's mom asked

Michael. "I left our car, and we've been using cabs. It would make things easier."

It could also be construed as aiding and abetting a fugitive, Liza thought.

Michael evidently had the same idea. "Are you sure this is a good idea?" he asked. "I don't know if Detective Quigley—"

"The detective told us not to leave town, and we haven't," Rikki said. "He has our cell phone numbers. If he wants us, he can call us. We'll come in." From the look on her face, that last idea didn't go down very comfortably.

Michael still tried to dodge. "It's not a big car, and with Liza's walker—"

"Liza and I could stay here while you get our stuff from the motel," Lolly volunteered. "We could go and have a burger in the same place where you and I had breakfast, Mom."

"Maybe that would be a good idea," Liza spoke up, surprising Michael and definitely not pleasing Rikki, who seemed determined to monitor everything her daughter said. "We'll just relax for a little and let you guys do the heavy lifting."

Rikki gave in with ill grace. Liza leaned against her walker as Michael and Lolly's mom set off back to dry land.

"So where's this burger place?" she asked.

Lolly led the way to a pleasant-looking little café on a side street. She declined a table on the outdoor patio for a booth inside.

Liza nodded in appreciation. Somewhere along the line, Lolly had picked up some basic anti-paparazzi training.

They sat down, and Lolly enthusiastically ordered the Swiss cheeseburger platter and an iced tea. Liza followed suit, adding a Diet Coke instead.

"Like that's going to help," she said wryly, making Lolly laugh.

"I know. I'm going way off my usual diet here," the young actress said after the waitress left. "Mom would kill me."

"We'll tell her we had the health salad," Liza promised. Lolly had definitely relaxed after Rikki left. With her mother around, Liza noticed that Lolly had barely gotten a word in edgewise.

Their orders arrived, and Lolly began making serious inroads on her burger and fries.

"Most folks outside the Business wouldn't think twice about ordering this." Liza took a bite from her own cheeseburger and held it up.

"Yeah, they see somebody like Forty Oz. partying at Café Tabú and figure that must be the life." Lolly took a sip of her tea. "They don't see the careful eating, or getting to bed at nine so you can be on the set at some ungodly hour for makeup call."

"Or kids taking classes during the downtime between filming scenes," Liza said. "That must have been like having two jobs at once."

Lolly nodded. "I spent a lot of time at boarding schools while Mom went abroad to make movies." She nibbled meditatively on the end of a French fry. "I think some of them she was kind of embarrassed over. No place to take a kid. When I started working, she insisted I only take U.S. projects. 'That's where you're going to make your career,' she'd say. I still don't have a passport."

"That's what happens sometimes with people who lead exciting lives," Liza said with a smile. "They know too well what can happen to their kids."

"It's always been Mom and me against the world." Lolly poured a little pond of catsup onto her plate for dipping her fries. "My dad died before I was born, you know."

"That's right." Hazy headlines about Lukas Popovic's death rose up in Liza's memory. "He was lost at sea."

"Mom says he always loved his sailboat." Lolly's fry consumption slowed down. "It was how he'd decompress after a project—climb aboard and go wherever the wind took him."

She gave Liza a bittersweet smile. "He and Mom got married on the boat. Dad pulled into some port in Mexico and got the local priest to hitch them. He was a monk in one of those brown robes with a hood. The mayor was this guy with a big black mustache. They just came aboard and did the ceremony. Sailing back to L.A. was their honeymoon, and then I came along. Mom was carrying me when Dad finished his next picture, and she didn't want to go sailing in her condition. Dad went anyway . . . and you know the rest."

Lolly looked silently at her plate for a moment. "Maybe having adventures isn't such a great thing."

They finished their meals in silence, lingering over their drinks after Liza had the waitress remove their plates. "Disposing of the evidence," she said, trying to lighten the mood.

But the word "evidence" obviously got Lolly thinking about her plight. "Do you believe me about the amnesia?" she asked abruptly, leaning across the table, her voice going low. "That detective obviously doesn't, and I can't talk to Mom about this."

"I do believe you." Lolly would have to be either the clone of Meryl Streep or a psychopath to carry off a deception of this magnitude. "And I know that head injuries can do strange things," she went on. "That can be taken to ridiculous extremes on TV and in the movies—"

"Soap operas," Lolly agreed with a wan smile.

"But it does happen." Liza dug out her cell phone. "I'm going to get on to my partner and see if her connections can come up with a good neurologist for you. Someone who might be able to explain the memory situation to you better"—she nodded toward the bandages hidden under Lolly's hat—"and who can look at those stitches for you. You won't be going back to the celebrity health care of Bel Air, will you?"

"I guess not." Lolly reached across the table to take Liza's hand before she could begin dialing. "And thanks for listening. You don't know how it feels, not being able to remember anything . . . especially when that means anything *could* have happened."

She looked at Liza, her eyes haunted. "How can I know?"

"Maybe the doctor can help," Liza said gently. "I understand that sometimes when the brain takes a shock, memories can come back in time on their own."

She gave Lolly's hand a gentle squeeze. "Until that happens—"

"Unless," Lolly said miserably.

"You can't know," Liza went on. "The only way you can deal with the uncertainty is to hope for the best. You have your mom on your side, and you have Michael and me, too."

Lolly's face took on the same expression Liza had seen a thousand times before—the gratitude of someone in trouble being bailed out.

This time, at least we're helping a fairly decent person, not some spoiled brat, Liza thought grimly. *I only hope we can make good on what I just promised.*

11

The cell phone lying disregarded in Liza's hand began to bleat. The caller ID showed Michelle Markson's name, so Liza made the connection. "I was just about to call you," she began.

"We need to meet." Michelle cut right over Liza's words. "I take it you're not in Michael's house, because my call there went to his answering system. How soon can you get here?"

"We're in Santa Monica, but Michael isn't with me right now."

"At least you're close enough to Century City. Please get here as soon as possible." Coming from Michelle, that meant "the day before yesterday."

Before her partner could hang up, Liza said, "There was a reason I was going to call you." In a low voice, she explained Lolly's problem.

"Amnesia?" Michelle's voice dripped with cynical disbelief. "And you believe her?"

"I'm having lunch with her," Liza diplomatically replied.

"So you can't answer my question in front of her face," Michelle said.

"No, I can do that," Liza said into her phone. "And the answer would be yes."

That left her with a brief silence from Michelle. "You always had this tendency toward kindheartedness," her partner finally said. "It made you popular with clients, but it can be a drawback in our business—makes it hard to read people."

"There is that," Liza said. "I guess we can discuss it when I see you."

"By which time I should probably have the name of someone to treat your friend." With her sources of information, Michelle would probably dig up a neurologist long before Liza and Michael made it to her office.

Liza thanked Michelle, who, as usual, clicked off in the middle.

"I'll be seeing Michelle later, so I should have a name for you afterward."

"Thanks." Lolly raised a careful hand to rub at the bandage under her hat. "This is getting kind of itchy."

Liza raised a hand to get their waitress. "Let's settle the bill so we'll be ready to roll."

No sooner did she send the server off with their payment and a tip than Liza saw Rikki Popovic enter the restaurant and head for their table. "Michael is waiting outside with the car," she reported.

As Liza labored her way out behind the Popovics, Lolly filled her mother in on the call to Michelle and the possibility of getting a new doctor that no one connected with *The Lowdown* would know about.

Reaching the door, Rikki went out first to check for the dreaded paparazzi. Turning back, she said, "Why don't you go first, Liza?"

Liza set off, accompanied by Rikki. "Thank you so much for your help with the doctor," the older woman said. "I'm worried and want Lolly to be looked at, but we can't go back to that place. If one of those camera people turned up today, four will be there tomorrow. They breed like lice."

She helped Liza get into the backseat and stowed the walker, then beckoned to Lolly, who quickly entered the front passenger's seat.

They didn't go too far, aiming for a nondescript motel about half a mile away.

Michael cruised past once while Rikki scoped out the street and parking lot for the enemy—especially the SUV serving as a hunting blind for the paparazzo who'd stalked them at the hospital.

"He's persistent," she said grimly. "What if he went to the dispatcher who sent the cab that brought us to the hospital? Then he could backtrack us to the last place where we were staying. He could even have followed us from there and gotten more people to wait for us here."

Michael sighed. "Rikki, I think you're getting paranoid."

"Did you see the way he went after my daughter?" Rikki demanded. "I just want to make sure that Lolly will be safe."

At last, even Rikki was satisfied. Michael pulled up in front of their room. Rikki got out. But before Lolly left, she leaned over, whispered something, and kissed Michael on the cheek.

As they drove away, Liza asked, "What did she say?"

" 'I'm glad my Mom knows such good people.' " Michael glanced back at Liza in the rear seat. "What did you do that polished up our halos so much?"

Liza shrugged and told him how she'd asked Michelle for help with finding a doctor for Lolly. "And by the way, we'd better get onto Santa Monica Boulevard again. Michelle is expecting us in Century City ASAP."

"Well, that just puts the cherry on top of my day," Michael said. "Dealing with Rikki, I knew she was giving me grief because she's just about out of her mind over her daughter. Michelle just gives me grief because it's her way of life."

Still muttering, he drove down the Boulevard into Century City. They pulled up in front of the building where Liza used to work, and Michael left the Honda's keys with a parking valet whose expression showed that he usually dealt with Beemers and Mercedes.

The guy's face just about went purple when Michael said, "Don't get it dirty," and then accompanied Liza into the lobby.

"Looks as if the place got a little shaken up in the quake." Liza nodded to one of the large windows where workmen were removing a piece of cracked plate glass.

"I'm sure we won't see anything upstairs," Michael assured her. "No way would Michelle let God mess up her office."

A brief elevator ride delivered them to the reception area of Markson Associates. Liza's eyes opened wide with delight when she saw who was sitting behind the enormous front desk.

"Ysabel! I thought I'd find one of those temps that Michelle delights in terrorizing."

The striking Latina came from behind the desk to give Liza a hug. "Haven't quit this week—yet."

Ysabel Fuentes would have the record as the longest-serving employee of Markson Associates. The receptionist not only knew the company's history but also had an encyclopedic knowledge of the clients and the film business in general. Ysabel also had a stormy relationship with Michelle, regularly quitting and then being wooed back—that had been part of Liza's job when she worked full-time.

In between, the front desk was manned by a succession of temps, most of whom barely lasted a day in proximity to the Markson take-no-prisoners style.

"The boss is in her office with Buck Foreman." Ysabel gave them a mischievous grin. "In conference, but not incommunicado."

Michelle had a habit of disappearing during quiet times,

cutting the cords that connected her to the agency. Liza and Ysabel had both noticed that Buck turned out to be unavailable at the same times.

The receptionist went back behind her desk. "I'll phone in and say you're here. Don't hurry—it only feeds her megalomania."

"Hurry?" Liza shook her walker. "With this?"

"Just shows the power of your personality," Ysabel said with a smile. "I didn't even notice it."

Liza humped the walker down familiar hallways to Michelle's office.

"It still baffles me how Ysabel manages to keep a job here—especially when she quits all the time," Michelle said.

Liza shrugged. "It helps when you know where all the bodies are buried."

She found the door to Michelle's office open. Buck Foreman sat on the oversized couch. Michelle stood in front of her desk, arms crossed and leaning one hip onto the desktop.

Before Liza could speak, Michelle stepped forward and gave her a piece of paper. "That's the number you wanted for Lolly Popovic. Now, as to why I asked you here . . ."

She turned to Buck, who held up a photo. "Based on the description you gave us, this is the guy who's been stalking Lolly?"

It looked like a publicity photo, but even though his lank hair had been artfully teased around, Liza recognized the paparazzo's high cheekbones, snub nose, and cleft chin.

"That's the guy," she said.

Michael nodded.

"He's Chester 'Chick' Benson," Buck reported with a grimly amused smile. "Apparently, he got the nickname because people think he looks like a chick."

"As in female." Michelle scrutinized the photo. "Well, he does have feminine features, which only makes me wonder about Ritz Tarleton's choice in men."

"You mean, this guy and Ritz—?" Michael broke off, stumbling over his own tongue.

"It shouldn't be that much of a surprise," Michelle told him. "After all, Britney hooked up with a paparazzo for a while."

"Talk about sleeping with the enemy," Liza said.

"Ritz and Chick managed to keep their connection under the radar," Buck reported. "They ate at burger joints—places were Ritz Tarleton normally wouldn't be found dead, pardon the phrase—or takeout. Also, Ritz would arrange for them to rendezvous at various vacant houses and apartments—vacant because her friends were out of town."

"Ummmmm . . . ick?" Liza ventured.

Michelle wrinkled her nose. "I hope they had the decency to launder the sheets afterward."

Buck just shrugged. "I wouldn't even have gotten a line on any of this, except one of her friends—ex-friends now—happened to come home unexpectedly and caught Ritz and a guy in the sack. The guy bailed out a window, but the friend got a glimpse of his face."

"And then recognized him as one of Don Lowe's stooges on *The Lowdown*," Michelle finished with a look of distaste.

"For a couple keeping up a supposedly secret relationship, they took plenty of big chances," Liza pointed out.

Buck shrugged again. "I wouldn't say discretion was one of Ms. Tarleton's strong points."

"Discretion, not so much," Michael agreed. "Thrill-seeking, on the other hand . . ."

"On the other hand, Ritz had as strong a reason to keep this on the down-low as some of the people she black-mailed," Liza said. "It would not help her fading rep as a hot celebrity babe for it to get out that she was boffing a—a—"

"A lower life-form like Chick Benson?" Michael suggested.

"I find myself wondering who initiated this liaison," Michelle said.

"Let's face it—Ritz had just about gotten to the point where she couldn't get arrested in this town," Buck pointed out.

"We kidded about her sleeping with the enemy, but it seems more like a symbiotic relationship." Michael spoke slowly, frowning in thought. "Chick could use Ritz to get access to her celebrity friends."

"And she could use him to drum up some sort of publicity for herself," Liza finished. "What I'd like to know is how long had this been going on?"

She looked over at Buck. "Do you have any line on their being together recently?"

The detective responded with a quick headshake. "Nothing after that time they almost got caught."

That got Michael's attention. "So either they went even farther under the radar—"

"If they tried, they'd have to go underground," Buck interrupted.

"Or they'd have had to break it off," said Michelle, taking it to the logical conclusion.

"That would explain Chick's bad attitude with Lolly," Michael suggested. "He's still PO'ed after being dumped."

"If there was dumping involved, that would probably be Ritz," Liza had to admit.

"That might explain his aggressive ambush style, but not the questions," Michelle disagreed. "He was trying to get Lolly Popovic to confess to murdering Ritz Tarleton. Sounds more like guilt to me."

Michael laughed. "You mean, 'Oh, if only we were still together, Ritz might not have come to such a terrible end'?"

Michelle gave him a dead serious look. "No, I mean that he might well have been the person who pushed Ritz back into that collapsing bungalow."

She paused at the look on his face. "Never underestimate

the power of rejected love." Michelle glanced over at Liza. "I would think you should realize that."

Thanks a lot, Michelle, Liza thought.

Michelle, however, didn't even notice the uncomfortable silence. "I think you should go and ask Chick Benson about it," she said.

The building that housed operations for *The Lowdown* was either less well constructed or considerably less lucky than Markson Associates' Century City digs. The wall by the entrance had a big crack, as if a large sledgehammer handled by an even larger person had landed in the middle of the marble panel.

Sitting in Michael's Honda, Liza kept staring at the crack. Was it getting larger?

I hope that's not a load-bearing wall, she found herself thinking.

Then she remembered the incident that had nearly brained Lolly Popovic, where a facade sheathing a building's front had fallen away and crashed to the street.

Was that crack getting bigger?

All of a sudden, the notion of staking out *Lowdown* HQ seemed less and less of a great idea.

Liza alternated between looking at her watch and glancing at that crack in the wall. She tried to console herself with the idea that one of them not moving was probably a good thing.

As the wait continued to stretch, however, she began to feel a new strain.

If this falls apart because I had to find a john, she silently groused, *I don't know who'll be more annoyed—Michelle or me.*

Then she spotted Chick Benson walking up the block.

Should I let him get closer? Liza decided to open the door. She slid out her walker, hoping the door panel would hide it from Benson's sight. Then she boosted herself out of her seat, ignoring the warning twinge her knee gave at all this enthusiastic movement.

Liza was up and on the sidewalk before Chick Benson noticed her.

Benson should have had no problem escaping from a woman with a walker—hell, he could probably have outrun Michael, who had just come out of the driver's side door.

But the paparazzo was just as shocked as all the people he regularly ambushed. Instead of running, he stood knock-kneed, his hands placed to block any possible shot at his crotch.

"Lady," he started, then stopped himself. "It's Liza, isn't it? Liza, you gotta stop taking all this stuff so personally."

"Yeah, it's funny how people react to guys like you taking pictures of their personal lives." Liza shoved her walker a step closer. "But this time I wanted to ask about *your* personal life—at least the part of it you spent with Ritz Tarleton."

For a second, Benson stood very still. Then his hands slid away to his sides, as if there were no hope of shielding anything.

"I guess I had to expect it would come out sooner or later." He let out a deep sigh. "It was fun while it lasted.

"Everyone made fun of her as if she was stupid," Benson said. "But she could be really smart, the way she talked people into doing things." His face softened a little in memory. "My Irish grandmother called it blarney. My Dad just called it BS. Ritz knew how to use it, and she stuck it to a lot of people."

"People who were supposed to be her friends," Liza pointed out.

"What friends?" Benson asked scornfully. "She hated most of 'em! To those guys, she was just a walking charge card. 'Oh, Ritz will pick it up!' " he mimicked in a falsetto voice and a dismissive wave of his hands.

"I saw her set up some big names beautifully—if she could do that, she had the chops to be a real actress."

Liza thought about Chard Switzer, Sukey Tupp, Samantha Pang . . . and maybe even Chick Benson. Ritz must have been very plausible to pull off the things she did.

Liza almost missed what Benson said next. "Lowe thought that was pretty funny."

"So Don Lowe knew about her?" Liza pounced. "She wasn't just setting up people for your camera?"

"He figured it out and busted us," Chick Benson admitted.

"And did Ritz dump you after that?" Michael asked.

"It's not like you're saying!" Benson flared. "We just hit bad times. A friend of hers almost caught us, and her old man cut off her money."

Liza nodded encouragingly. That tied in with what Fritz Tarleton had said.

"I told her she could move in with me," Chick went on. "I'm, like, one of the only guys from my film school class who's actually making regular money. But Ritz said if people knew we were together, Lowe wouldn't have any use for us. And she needed the money he paid her to live on."

"So she was actually setting people up so Don Lowe could get embarrassing footage of them." Michael wanted to be sure about what Benson was saying.

"Like Sukey Tupp?" Liza added.

Benson's lips twisted. "That skank always acted like she was so much better than Ritz. She was a real singer, and Ritz wasn't. But if Ritz had some blow, that was plenty good enough for old Sukey. I didn't mind helping to take her down one little bit."

Liza looked at him carefully. "Did you know that filming Sukey falling off the wagon so publicly set things up so that Ritz could be on *D-Kodas*?"

Chick blinked in surprise. "It did?"

Michael lost patience. "Come on, she had some scam

going on the set there. That's probably why she got herself killed."

The shock and surprise that showed on Benson's face looked pretty genuine to Liza, but Michael evidently wasn't sure. "You're going to tell me you didn't know anything about it? Or maybe that was the problem—you learned that Ritz was cutting you out."

The young paparazzo's girlish features were white, his lank hair hanging in his eyes. "I don't know what you're talking about. Ritz caught me at the Atotori Studios gate and told me to stay away from there. But it's not like you say."

Michael didn't let up. Liza wondered if he was channeling a tough cop from one of his scripts—or was this what he was like when he really cared about something?

"Maybe you don't know what I'm talking about," he pressed on. "The question is, did you do what Ritz told you? Did you stay away? Where were you when the quake hit, Benson? Can you prove it?"

12

"You think that *I* killed Ritz?" Chick Benson burst out. "You guys must be even crazier than I thought."

"Actually, we try pretty hard to be rational," Michael said calmly. "That's why we're asking you to prove that you were somewhere else."

"Well I hate to bust your bubble, but I can do that," the paparazzo responded angrily. "When the earthquake hit, I was out in Malibu, getting some footage of Brant Lee cheating on his fiancée."

"I can't say much about Brant Lee's acting, but he looks pretty good shirtless," Liza observed.

"He was shirtless right down to his toenails, bailing out of a hot tub when the ground began to shake," Benson told her.

"Wait a second—Brant Lee is engaged to that country singer, Andi Flanders. She's a babe! Who could be worthwhile for him to be cheating with?"

"Would you believe her kid sister Jenna?" Chick replied, obviously relishing a gossip journalist's dream.

Michael shook his head. "God, this is like one of those really cheesy decadent Hollywood novels."

"Jackie Collins or Jacqueline Suzanne?" Liza asked.

"I'm thinking much earlier, back to something Wilson Mizner said," Michael replied. "He compared Hollywood to riding through a sewer in a glass-bottomed boat."

"Who's Wilson Mizner?" Benson asked.

"One of the original partners in the Brown Derby," Michael explained.

The paparazzo gave him an "Are you kidding me?" look. "He went in with other people to buy a hat?"

"The Brown Derby was a restaurant—several restaurants, where the stars all hung out in the thirties and forties." Michael ran down when he saw Chick Benson shrug.

"I'm into news," the paparazzo said, "not ancient history."

"Well, now I'm feeling ancient," Michael muttered.

"We're missing the point, people." Liza glared at Benson. "What we're trying to get here is a solid alibi."

"And I just gave it to you," Benson retorted. "Brant Lee made a spectacle of himself because of the earthquake. You can see it on camera. The water in the hot tub was sloshing around in the tremor."

"The only way we could check that is by actually looking at what you shot," Liza said.

Benson shrugged. "It's upstairs in the office. You want to go up there and ask the boss?"

"Yeah, let's do that." Michael took a step toward the entrance, only to be halted by Chick Benson's upraised hand.

"If the lady wants to talk to the boss, that's one thing. He doesn't do delegations."

"Maybe you want to stay with the car," Liza said to Michael in an undertone. "That's not a legal spot. You could get towed."

Michael made a rude noise, but he kept it low. "I suppose you know what you're doing."

He stomped back to the Honda as Liza wielded her walker after Chick Benson.

After following him into the elevator, Liza watched the

paparazzo punch a button. They rode up in silence—
nervous silence on Liza's part, since the elevator car's
movement was a bit jerky. She really wanted to ask if it had
moved the same way before the quake, but decided it was
better to keep her mouth shut.

The doors opened on a nondescript hallway.

*I guess Don Lowe doesn't feel the need to waste money
on ambience,* Liza thought.

But a fair amount of money had gone into the barrier
blocking access to the one entrance door. Lowe hadn't
wasted money on a receptionist, either—two hefty security guards stood ready to defend the chest-high barricade.
They nodded at Chick, and then turned hard eyes on Liza,
demanding to know her business.

For a brief moment, Liza wondered if Benson had suck-
ered her. Would he just breeze through, leaving her to hang
in the wind (or dangle from the grip of one of the uni-
formed behemoths)?

But Benson pointed to the phone behind the barrier,
saying, "I have to talk to the big guy."

The guard punched in a four-digit extension and handed
the receiver to Chick.

"I've got Liza Kelly in reception," he reported into the
phone. "She knows stuff."

Benson returned the phone to the guard, who listened
and then buzzed in both Liza and the paparazzo.

Chick skirted the edges of the large bullpen area where
most of the staff congregated (and, Liza realized, where
the show was actually recorded).

He led the way down a long hallway with fairly pokey
offices on either side, but it ended in a space that was both
large and opulently furnished.

Don Lowe sat behind a desk that had to take up at least
as much room as Michael's Honda. He rose, a short, burly
man with craggy features and heavy eyebrows, wearing
the same white shirt he usually wore during his show, open

at the throat, the sleeves rolled up over meaty forearms. Lowe nodded to Chick Benson, and then said, "Well, hello, Ms. Kelly. We don't get many visitors here."

"From the looks of your security setup, I'd say it's more a case of you actively discouraging visitors," Liza told him. "But then, I guess a lot of people might want to have words with you these days."

Lowe shrugged, those heavy eyebrows rising in time with his shoulders. "There it is. I can't depend on anonymity anymore—not that I'm complaining, you understand. To steal an old quote, 'Gossip has been berry, berry good to me.'"

He gestured to a chair and sat down himself. Chick Benson remained standing in the doorway. "So, what can I do for you?"

"You could confirm some information I was discussing with your employee."

"Oh, yes, the 'stuff' Chick mentioned on the phone." Lowe gave Liza a measuring gaze. "I don't know why I should answer any questions. You're not a journalist."

Liza kept herself from responding, "Are you?" Instead, she settled in the overly soft guest chair and said, "So you invited me back here to say no to my face? It would have been easier just telling the guards to toss me out on my keister."

"I was curious," Don Lowe said. "A journalist's failing, I guess."

"Well, I'll try to satisfy that curiosity," Liza told him. "I want to help a young friend who seems to be in danger of being set up as the only possible suspect for Ritz Tarleton's murder—by a whole bunch of so-called journalists."

Lowe nodded, his face still noncommittal.

"We—some friends and I—figured out the relationship between Ritz and Mr. Benson here. When he saw we could back up that supposition with some facts, he admitted their connection, admitted that she had helped to set up some

shots for him . . . and then slipped up by mentioning that
she ended up doing the same for you."

That earned Chick a rather cold glance from his boss. "I
suppose he's more used to asking embarrassing questions
than answering them."

Lowe's eyes took on a calculating gleam. Then he nodded. "You want me to confirm that Ritz was a regular
source? Off the record, yes."

Liza stared, amazed at the gossipmonger's nerve. "You
were paying her to arrange stories for you?"

"Is it all that different when a tabloid pays for someone's criminal or health records?" Lowe asked her back.
"It's just another kind of checkbook journalism."

"But she actually set people up in embarrassing situ-
ations for your cameras to catch. Isn't that entrapment?"

"There are shows on cable, and even network TV,
devoted to punking celebrities. Isn't that essentially the
same thing?" Lowe shrugged. "I don't see what Ritz did as
trapping people—more like testing them. If the cops can
use informants to nail drug dealers, why can't we use the
same techniques to find out how good our supposed role
models really are?"

Liza shook her head. "I don't know how much of a role
model Sukey Tupp might be—except maybe for delin-
quents. What does getting her to fall off the wagon prove?"

"Maybe that she should have stayed in rehab longer,"
Lowe shot back.

Now it was Liza's turn to study Lowe's rough-hewn but
still attractive features. He seemed to have an answer for
everything. Maybe it was time to stop questioning his eth-
ics and concentrate on Ritz. "Did you know that putting
Sukey back into rehab would also open a spot for Ritz in
the *D-Kodas* Celebrity Week?"

Lowe took a moment to respond. "That was a surprise,"
he admitted. "It was naughty of little Ritz to feather her

own nest that way." He looked like a father explaining a bit of mischief by his three-year-old.

"So you had nothing going on that required Ritz to be on the set of the show?"

"Like what?" Lowe asked. "Wish Dudek is old news. His divorce is—what? Ten years ago now? As for Darrie Brunswick, well, it's almost as long since those shots from her early career as a lingerie model resurfaced."

He settled back in his plush seat, his big, dark eyebrows lazily rising. "We keep hearing rumors about a nude photo set, but that's more a thing for the men's magazines than for us."

"Ritz was up to something during her time on *D-Kodas*," Liza said. "And if it wasn't for your show, then she was really feathering her nest, wasn't she?"

Lowe's indulgent expression faded, replaced by the face of a hard-nosed journalist. "So what was she doing, Ms. Kelly?"

Liza gave him back one of his annoying shrugs. "Frankly, I came here to find out from you," she admitted. "Ritz told a friend she was working on something big—something really good for her. But it seems that neither you nor Mr. Benson knows what that was."

She glanced over her shoulder at Chick, who looked bereft.

Maybe his true love wasn't so truthful to him, Liza thought.

Don Lowe, on the other hand, looked like a hungry lion who'd just had a bloody steak snatched out from under his nose.

I thought he'd be harder to read than that, Liza thought. *But then, journalists are competitive by nature. One thing's for sure. Our friend Mr. Lowe isn't as easy as he let on about sources going off on their own agendas.*

Liza tried a few more minutes of fencing but could see that she wasn't going to get any more information.

"One thing I'd like," she said. "Could I get a look at what Chick was shooting during the earthquake?"

She tried to be diplomatic, not using words like "allegedly."

Lowe's poker face took over, but then he said, "I don't suppose it would hurt if you looked at the raw footage—after signing an appropriate nondisclosure form, of course."

After carefully parsing the legalese, Liza added her signature. *At least he didn't ask for it in blood,* she thought as Lowe dismissed her into Chick Benson's care. The paparazzo led her into a fairly impressive editing suite, fired up a screen, and hit a couple of buttons. A couple cavorting in a hot tub swam into focus.

"Okay," a voice easily recognizable as Chick's muttered on the audio track. "Let's see if I can get both faces and no boobs."

The two people in the tub were involved in a long kiss, and all Chick could get was the back of the male's head blocking the woman's face.

"They gotta come up for air sometime," he groused.

Then the camera jerked away from the kissing pair, going out of focus on a view of a carefully tended lawn.

"Dammitall!" Benson recovered and got the camera back on the tub. Just as he'd told Liza, the water was sloshing around and the man was making a panicked exit. Liza was distracted by some of the bits dangling in the breeze, but Chick managed to bring the camera up to get a clear shot of the man's face. Definitely Brant Lee.

"I guess I can see your problem," she said. "Too much of him on camera."

"We could pixelate the naughty bits enough to meet network standards," Benson disgustedly told her. "The problem is the jackass wasn't a gentleman. Instead of helping Jenna out, he dithered around, blocking her face."

True enough. Lee's usual on-screen persona was either heroic or soulful. He didn't look either in this scene, his face slack with fear as he bounced from foot to foot trying to decide what to do. What he did accomplish, probably quite unintentionally, was to keep his nude torso between his companion's face and the candid cameraman.

The woman must have yelled at him, because Brant finally moved, circling the tub to help her out. But now her back was to the camera. All Chick got was a shot of a very cute butt wiggling its way toward a bathhouse in the distance.

Again the camera jerked.

The aftershock, Liza thought.

This time, Benson came out with a "Whoa!" and some colorful cursing as the camera showed foliage and a tree trunk.

Liza turned to the cameraman. "You were up in a tree during the earthquake? Didn't it occur to you that you might have fallen out and broken your neck?"

"Not until later," Benson admitted. Liza wasn't sure whether his look of embarrassment came from a belated sense of danger or disappointment over not catching his quarry.

"I kept hoping I could get the shot." He sighed. "But you see, there was nothing we could use."

Liza stopped by Don Lowe's office to thank him—a publicist's rather than a journalist's move. No sense in burning a bridge she might want to revisit with more ammunition.

She heaved her walker along after Chick Benson until they were back at the security checkpoint. Then she headed down in the elevator alone.

Michael just about flew over to the door when he saw Liza coming out. "Well?"

"I'll tell you everything," Liza promised, "on the way home. All of a sudden, I feel very, very tired."

As Michael drove back to Westwood, Liza reported her conversation with Don Lowe and the outtakes from Chick Benson's camera.

"You could definitely hear Benson's voice," she finished.

"Plus you see the earthquake—and Brant Lee naked and trashing his public image. The earthquake might have been faked, but I don't think Mr. Lee would do much in the way of a favor for Chick."

"With an alibi like that, it looks as if Benson was a pretty short-lived suspect," Michael said, coming up to their driveway.

"But we still have Don Lowe," Liza pointed out as Michael opened the door for her. She got out her walker and headed for the house. "I didn't want to put him on his guard by asking where he was during the quake. But once we get inside, I'm going to sic Buck Foreman on him. He'll see what kind of alibi Lowe has—if he's got one."

Liza was as good as her word. The first thing she did on getting into the living room was to call Buck.

"This may take a while," he warned after she told him what she wanted. "Like a lot of people who specialize in invading people's privacy, Lowe is very protective of his own."

"I know you'll do your best—and I'm betting that will be more than enough," Liza told him. "Unless he really has something to hide."

She hung up and then turned to Michael, who'd been running through messages on voice mail. Most of them he just skipped through. But then Liza heard a familiar voice.

"Hey, this is Ava." Liza's editor from the *Oregon Daily* sounded her usual slightly rushed, managing-editor self.

But then Ava switched over to her best-friend mode for a moment. "Kind of weird to call you at your old home. I hope you remember us up here in Maiden's Bay—especially since your cushion is getting mighty thin." Somewhere in the middle there, Ava had gone back to her professional persona again.

Liza and Michael shared a look.

"Message received," she said, scooping up her papers from the couch and sitting on the seat. "I'm back at work."

Within an hour, Liza had cleaned up the puzzles she'd been working on and drafted another one.

Michael came around to peek over her shoulder. "Wow, you're just churning them out."

Stung, she shot him a challenging look. "You got a problem? Try one and see."

But Michael shook his head. "Sorry; I'm working on one already—it's a download from my phone."

It took Liza a moment to remember. "That's one of the puzzles Lolly sent you? The ones she got from Ritz? How are they?"

"I also got a couple from Samantha Pang while I was waiting in the car for you," Michael said.

Liza recalled the math girl's comment. "She said they didn't make any sense."

Michael handed her one sheet of paper—a clean copy of a sudoku puzzle.

7						9	3	2
	2	3	5					
		7		9				
	3		1					9
	4		8		5			
	5			7			8	
	3	9			2	8	4	
			8		7			
		6						

"Well, I solved this one. It was kind of messy."

Liza frowned as she scanned the array of numbers. "I see what you mean. For a start, it's not symmetrical."

Symmetry—duplicating the pattern of clues either from side to side, top to bottom, or even on the diagonal—was highly prized among aficionados of classic sudoku. It didn't have to be a mirror image—sometimes puzzle builders twisted the pattern around.

But this puzzle, as Michael said, was a mess. The numbers in the grid clotted together seemingly at random.

"Considering how poorly she did in my class, I guess I should be glad Ritz managed to construct a puzzle at all," Liza finally said.

"Well, you won't be so glad to see this one." Michael gave her the other sheet—another hodgepodge of a puzzle.

Liza's frown deepened as she looked at it. "This one definitely doesn't work," she said.

"You saw it, huh?" Michael's finger ran across the three subgrids on the bottom of the puzzle. "Three threes in a row—and two of them almost side by side. It's printed out in Solv-a-Doku style, but it looks as if she didn't even use the program to check her work."

Liza looked from puzzle to puzzle, more baffled by the discrepancy than she usually was by the most carefully crafted sudoku.

"If Ritz constructed a puzzle that worked," Liza muttered, rattling one sheet of paper, "how could she go on to create one with such an obvious defect?"

Michael's answering frown lightened into a look of reminiscence.

"Remember the case you stepped into the last time you came down to sunny California?" he asked. "One of the murder victims hid a number to remember by jotting down the digits on a sudoku puzzle. You noticed it because she filled in the wrong spaces."

"I remember—not necessarily fondly," Liza told him. She poked at the failed puzzle as if it might blow up.

"So you're suggesting that this is some sort of . . . message?"

13

After another meal of takeout—pizza this time—Liza sat in front of Michael's miniature budget laptop, silently cursing the tiny keyboard and that funny little pad that was supposed to take the place of a mouse. It never worked for her; she always wound up typing gibberish because she was used to a human-sized keyboard.

But no, Michael had been determined to prove that he could be fiscally prudent—or as he said at the time, "I don't want to buy this with Michelle Markson's money."

Come to think of it, that was probably the first intimation that things weren't exactly copasetic between Michael and me, Liza thought.

And she was still annoyed over that long-ago argument.

Focus, she scolded herself. *You're letting yourself get distracted.*

Leaning over the keyboard, she played with the touchpad, went online, called up her account, and clicked on instant messages. Picking the recipient she wanted, she began typing.

Hey, Uncle Jim. Are you there? It's after eight in the evening

here in Pacific Daylight Time, and Japan doesn't do daylight savings, so I figure it has to be 10 something in the morning where you are.

"Damn keyboard," Liza muttered as she read over her typing.

On the bright side, however, she got an almost immediate response.

The letters appeared on the laptop screen.

Good to hear from you, Liza. Your timing is good, I just got into the office. So, is this a friendly Internet chat, or are you going to pick my brains?

Uncle Jim Watanabe's office was in the U.S. embassy in Tokyo, where he supposedly worked as a low-level communications specialist. But, given his lifelong interest in sudoku and codes, Liza had her suspicions. Japan stood right on Russia's doorstep, a perfect vantage point for signals intelligence—whether from an evil empire or a democratic federation.

Maybe it was a romantic notion, but Liza believed her uncle Jim was a spy.

Brain-picking, she admitted as she typed. **I thought you'd gotten interested in the notion of hiding a message in a sudoku and wondered if you had any new ideas on how to do it.**

I've gotten news of several sudoku-related cases that you managed to crack without any help from me. Liza read that with a frown. Was Uncle Jim pleased with her success or not?

I was able to tease out some numbers hidden in puzzles, she typed. **But this is a situation where I think an actual message may be stashed in a puzzle.**

She gave the background on the celebrity *D-Kodas* competition and Ritz Tarleton's demise, along with the fact that Ritz had sent sudoku to potential blackmail victims.

Some of the puzzles worked, some didn't—illegal numbers appearing side by side. Michael remembered a case where something similar had happened in the answers to a puzzle—

You're back with Michael? Uncle Jim interrupted.

He's helped me on several cases, and I'm staying in our old place in Westwood until the people on the show decide what to do. h45urt My Knee and wanted to stay with someone.

"Great typing," she sarcastically complimented herself.

It took so long for Uncle Jim to reply that Liza wondered if their connection had been cut. Finally letters appeared on the screen.

I always liked Michael, although that's not the same as living with him. Tell me more about these puzzles.

I can send them to you. Liza arranged the downloaded puzzles as attachments for an e-mail and sent them to her uncle. Then she went back to the IM link and typed up her theory that the puzzles were, to an extent, time bombs—innocent-looking packages that contained a message to be decoded later. She sighed as she saw the snarled spelling when her fingers got ahead of her brain—and wandered around the tiny keyboard.

When she finished, she wondered if what she'd sent had made any sense. And it didn't reassure her that she faced another long space of empty screen. Finally Uncle Jim typed, **Liza, placing hidden messages has to be a two-way street. Both message-sender and receiver must have a key to translate the code.**

We've talked about some kinds of codes involving numbers. There's the number for letter transposition, where 1=A, 2=B, etc. There are also ways an encoder can mix things up a little so the message is harder to crack.

The problem with sudoku is that there are only 9 digits—makes it hard to present 26 letters.

Now it's possible to use a book code in a sudoku. Suppose the first three clues or the first three answer spaces contain a 4, 9, and 2. The person receiving the message would turn to the page 4 of an agreed-on book, go down to line 9, and read the second word—which would become the first word of the message. Then on to the next three spaces or clues. Since we see that the clues are fouled up in several of the puzzles, it's

possible that they have a message encoded. But I'm afraid that deciphering the message would be impossible unless we knew that these three people had a book in common.

Liza blinked, trying to remember if she'd seen Ritz, Lolly, and Sam Pang even reading, much less the same book.

Wait a second—they all must have gotten the same briefing book from the D-Kodas producers that I did, she thought, then shook her head. The inches-thick binders would make pretty unwieldy codebooks.

Still, she passed along the idea to Uncle Jim, who suggested that she try comparing groups of three clues to words in the book.

If you start getting something intelligible, you'll have cracked the code, he typed.

I suspect you won't be holding your breath, Liza typed back.

Uncle Jim's reply appeared on the screen. **I'm sure it would take a while. And I have to admit, it's not a sure thing.**

The only thing that makes a code possible is that the person receiving the information knows how to decipher it. From what you're saying, it seems neither Lolly Popovic nor Samantha Pang got the key.

They spent a little more time on the IM connection— Uncle Jim had a lot of questions about Michael—but it was just chitchat, nothing more to do with sudoku. Liza's uncle did wish her good luck before they ended the session.

Michael looked up expectantly when Liza joined him on the couch. "From the look on your face, you didn't get the magic spell to wring a message out of those puzzles," he said.

She gave him the gist of her chat with her uncle.

Michael's eyes lit up. "A book code! Did you bring that binder along?"

They went into her room, Michael carrying the mysterious sudoku. Liza dug out the briefing binder.

"You want to call out the numbers or page through the book?" she asked.

"I'll do the numbers, since I've got the puzzles already," he replied. "What do you think? Clues first, or answers?"

"Clues," Liza decided. "Since they're messed up, that suggests they're where the message is."

Michael nodded. "Content forcing the puzzle to change. Okay. Here's one with a mistake." He peered at the puzzle for a moment, then said, "One, seven, four."

Liza opened the binder. "The first page is a letter. Do I count the letterhead and the address as separate lines?"

"Try it that way," Michael suggested. "What do you get as the seventh line?"

"It's the first paragraph." Liza read aloud:

"'I'm delighted over your agreement to participate in the *D-Kodas* annual celebrity competition. The information in this packet should bring you up to speed.'"

She frowned. "The seventh line is the one beginning 'the *D-Kodas.*' So the fourth word is . . . 'should'?"

"Except for the opening of 'Auld Lang Syne,' I've never heard a sentence begin with 'should,'" Michael said. "Maybe it's the seventh line in the body of the letter?"

"That's the end—it's a pretty short letter," Liza told him. She counted down and read, "'. . . you have any questions.' That's the fourth word—'questions.'"

"Not a promising start," Michael said dubiously. "Let's try the next one."

They gave up on the direct approach when they got "questions executive Goodman."

"The Goodman referred to there is a quiz-show producer who died years ago," Michael said. "Are there any other Goodmans involved in *D-Kodas*?"

Liza ran down the list of producers, on-screen talent, and crew. "Not a Goodman in the place."

"I guess we can ask Sam Pang if she knows somebody named Goodman." Michael did not sound particularly confident.

"Apparently, an executive named Goodman, who should

be questioned, or has questions . . . or maybe we're not doing this right."

They tried starting from the other end of the puzzle, then reversing the order of the clues—word, line, page. They even switched to another puzzle. But all they got were nonsensical collections of words.

"I sort of like 'love her globes,' " Michael said.

Liza gave him a look. "You would. The problem is, it doesn't sound like much of a message, much less blackmail that someone would kill over."

"We're missing something," Michael agreed. "Maybe it's every third clue, or only even numbers, or—"

"Since we don't have the key, we'll never figure it out," Liza said gloomily. "Especially since the key may have died with Ritz."

She shook her head. "Maybe these are just what they are—sloppy puzzles. Why would Ritz send a message without the code?"

"Ritz may look foxy," Michael began, only to stop at another look from Liza. "No, not sexy, but literally like a fox with those sharp features."

"Uh-huh," Liza said with a dangerous amount of disbelief.

"What I'm saying is that Ritz looked like a fox—but she acted more like a cat. You know how they like to play with their food."

Now Liza was completely lost. "Come again?"

"I forget you never had a cat."

"Dad was a dog person," Liza said.

"Well, my mom had a cat. She'd corner a mouse, let it almost escape, then pounce on it again."

"The cat or your mom?" Liza couldn't help asking.

That earned her a look from Michael. "Turning the subject back to Ritz, I'm not sure if she had a personality flaw for messing with people, or if it might have been her idea of psychological warfare—softening up a blackmail victim or wearing her down."

He leaned forward, making his case. "Chard and Forty Oz. both were pretty close to her—Ritz had probably done something like this to them in the past. Neither Samantha Pang nor Lolly had spent much time with Ritz. Maybe the messages—if that's what they were—were supposed to confuse them and freak them out a little. Then, when the time was right, they'd get the code key—and maybe be more freaked-out."

He rested back against the pillows. "If I were writing her as a character, based on observation, I could see her developing that way."

"Meaning exactly what?" Liza said.

Michael shrugged. "In the limited time I spent with her, Ritz acted like a snotty little witch, but with a real talent for poking hard at people's sore spots."

Liza nodded. "Lolly's ethnic and personal background, Sam Pang's whole wallflower thing—"

"And my position on the Hollywood totem pole," Michael finished for her. "As for the big blowup you described, Darrie Brunswick has to be aware that the things she wears on the show have become part of the American jokebook. You can't call those costumes designer creations."

"More like designer debacles," Liza said.

"I mean, would you see yourself going into a store and saying, 'I want something like the gown Darrie Brunswick was wearing last Thursday'?"

"Not if I were sober and of sound mind," Liza replied with a laugh. Then she got quiet.

"Liza, please tell me you're not thinking of a Darrie Brunswick outfit you actually liked," Michael nervously tried to joke.

She shook her head. "I'm thinking that we ignored two more suspects. The last time I saw Darrie, she was screaming at Ritz." All traces of levity deserted Liza's expression. "And, of course, there's Wish."

Michael took her hand. "It's no fun, suspecting a friend."

"Or a friend's daughter," Liza agreed heavily. "But we have to ask."

She went to the phone and punched in Wish Dudek's number. A teenaged voice answered, getting a little more circumspect when she discovered an unknown caller.

"Could you tell your dad it's Liza Kelly? I'm a friend of his."

"Oh, yeah, you were supposed to be on the show." The young girl excused herself.

After a few seconds of dead air, Wish came on. "Liza? What's up? Did you get tired of the room service in Westwood?"

"I was thinking maybe we should have lunch," Liza said.

"Sure. Tomorrow good for you? I'm always happy to have a meal with a beautiful woman." He paused for a beat, then said, "Not the smartest thing to say for a guy who already has one divorce on his record."

But Liza heard laughter in the background. "Sounds as if you got off the hook, Romeo."

Wish added some laughter of his own. "The machinery is still rumbling on the Celebrity Week front, but I can ask some questions in the morning," he said. "Maybe I can get you an early report."

"That would be great," Liza said.

He's putting himself out for me, she thought. *No need to rain on the parade this early.* Aloud, she added, "Can we make it a reservation for three? I can't drive with this knee, so I'm depending on Michael. It would only be fair to include him—"

"And, I suppose, having your husband along will silence some of the wagging gossip tongues in this town." Wish laughed again.

They set the time and place—one thirty in a quiet place in the Valley.

Pretty well off the beaten path for autograph seekers and paparazzi, Liza thought.

A little more convivial back-and-forth, and then she hung up.

"How nice of you to you ensure my cooperation," Michael teased from his spot on the sofa.

"Oh, it was the least I could do," Liza kidded back.

"Probably the *very* least." He drew himself up with a mock-severe look on his face.

"What? Are you jealous?"

Michael opened his mouth—and then closed it, slumping a little in the seat and shutting down his whole playful air.

"I guess I am," he said quietly, sounding a little surprised at himself.

They sat in uncomfortable silence for a while, until Michael finally asked, "Do you want to watch some TV?"

"Yeah—yeah, that sounds good."

Liza winced. *Not too quick on the agreement,* she scolded herself.

Michael picked up the remote and turned on the set. After twenty seconds of channel surfing, he stopped clicking. "*The Lowdown* is coming on. Wanna watch?"

"Why not?" Liza replied. "We can watch them root around in someone else's dirty laundry."

The show started with the usual montage of celebrity shots, paparazzi, and, of course, Don Lowe's walking shot, followed by his acolytes. Usually, it switched to the bullpen, Lowe up front with a whiteboard, his paparazzi spread among the desks, pitching stories.

This time, however, the opening showed a close-up of Ritz Tarleton's face with Lowe doing a voice-over.

"All of Los Angeles felt the earthquake mere days ago. Thousands were injured, several killed. But Hollywood is haunted by the murder of Ritz Tarleton."

Then, all of a sudden, a close-up of Liza appeared on the screen as Lowe went on. "But now, someone else is haunting Hollywood—Liza Kelly, a puzzle expert who does a big side business in crime solving . . . especially murder."

Then Lowe went on to outline Liza's theory about the crime, adding, "After alienating everyone on the set of the game show, what did Ritz Tarleton hope to achieve—and how did it get her killed?"

The show went to commercial, but Liza kept staring at the screen until Michael physically turned her head to look at him.

"Liza, say something," he told her, "even if it's cursing and swearing. 'Cause otherwise, I'm afraid your head's about to explode."

14

The next morning, Liza still had a splitting headache as she paced up and down in the reception area of Michelle Markson's office. Well, at least she attempted to pace—it wasn't easy to accomplish with a walker.

It hadn't helped that it had been a morning—and evening—for screaming. Hal Quigley had called her before the end of the next segment on *The Lowdown*.

Liza was just as glad the cop was on the phone. She figured he'd look pretty ugly, what with all the froth coming out of his mouth.

Quigley had threatened arrest, interrogation, and possibly incarceration on Devil's Island. Liza had argued that yet again she hadn't hindered the police investigation; she'd been looking in places where Quigley hadn't. Had he known about the connection between Ritz Tarleton and Chick Benson? That had led her to talk with Don Lowe. If Quigley had a problem, he should take it up with the boss of *The Lowdown*.

No sooner had she gotten rid of Quigley than the phone rang again—this time with an aggravated Ava Barnes.

Ava didn't mince words. "If you have theories to share with a media outlet, maybe it should be the newspaper that pays you rather than some syndicated gossip show."

But when they went over the story, there was a great deal of hypothesis and very little in the way of fact. It came down to two news items: that Ritz was involved with Chick Benson and that she was working for Don Lowe.

"Which Lowe confirmed for you, but off the record, so we can't use it," Ava said grimly.

"Yeah. I noticed he didn't use it in his own broadcast."

"Why would he give away the existence of his secret weapon to people who'd only use it as an excuse to sue him?" Ava asked.

"On the other hand," she went on, "when you talked to Lowe, you didn't put it off the record."

"I was asking him questions," Liza protested.

Ava repressed a sigh—almost. "You didn't think he might turn them around and use them as statements?"

"Um—no." Now Liza was glad she hadn't bolstered her theory by actually quoting the people who'd been black-mailed. Doubtless, Lowe would happily have thrown them into the gossip barbecue pit. *I can't tell Ava, either,* she realized. *I promised Forty Oz. and Sam Pang I would keep their blackmail secret.*

"Which leaves the romantic connection between Ritz Tarleton and this paparazzo," Ava said.

"C'mon, Ava, that's a story more suited to the *National Interloper* than the *Oregon Daily.*"

"Most days, I wish we had the *Interloper*'s circulation," Ava responded gloomily as they concluded their conversation.

Okay, that had involved embarrassment more than scream-ing. When the summons to Michelle's office had arrived the next morning, Liza wasn't sure what to expect.

Not even Ysabel could offer an inkling of what Michelle had in mind.

"She did put in a call to Buck Foreman." The reception-ist tried to put a joking spin on the news. "I'm not sure if he's supposed to add moral support or help her dispose of any bodies."

In fact, Buck had already been closeted with Michelle when Liza and Michael arrived.

At least they faced no yelling when they went down the hallway. A guy as big as Buck didn't need to, and Michelle was famous for maintaining a quiet, almost conversational tone as she tore strips off people.

They entered to find Buck in his usual place on the office couch and Michelle behind her desk. "It seems," she said as Liza maneuvered her walker through the door, "that since you left this office you've gotten a bit fuzzy on what we do here. We're supposed to manage and control news coverage, not broadcast it willy-nilly."

Liza gripped the handles on her walker. This might be one of the rare occasions when Michelle really exploded.

Her partner took a deep breath, then released it in a rush. "And we especially don't do that with media upstarts like Don Lowe."

Another deep breath, and then Michelle asked, "How did it happen?"

Liza reported her conversation with Lowe, not bother-ing to sit down.

If you're going to be called on the carpet, you might as well stand, she told herself.

At the end of the recital, Michelle sat silent for a moment. "So, because you failed to mention three little words—well, I suppose 'off the record' is two little words and a medium-sized one—Lowe was able to trumpet your entire discus-sion all over the country. I hope this is a lesson to you."

"It wasn't our entire discussion," Liza said. "He held

back on the fact that Ritz and Chick were an item—and that he was paying Ritz to set people up for ambush journalism."

"If you can characterize what *The Lowdown* does as 'journalism.'" Michelle's tone remained acid, but at least she'd stopped directing it solely at Liza.

"I didn't tell Lowe anything I hadn't already told Detective Quigley," Liza tried to defend herself.

"But Quigley wasn't likely to syndicate it all over the country," Michelle responded. "Not to mention this market. It's like advertising your investigation to the murderer."

Liza's shoulders slumped a little. "Not that we've had all that many people to try and pin the murder on," she admitted. "Every time we get someone, they turn out to have an alibi."

Turning to Buck, she said, "Please tell me you've managed to get something on Don Lowe. Then he'd have a real reason to try to screw up the investigation."

But Buck shook his head.

"Lowe was having a high-profile Hollywood lunch at the Atrium."

"A very high-profile luncheon spot," Liza agreed gloomily.

"I've got at least five eyewitnesses, staff and patrons, who recognized Lowe. He was there during the earthquake." Buck's usually expressionless face took on a sardonic smile. "There's also a security camera that got some wonderful candid shots of Lowe knocking several people over in his hurry to get away from the tall building."

Michelle got to her feet, purring, "We may not be able to put him away, but I wonder whether one of the other tabloid TV shows might be interested in that footage."

Michael spoke up for the first time since they entered the office. "Speaking of lunch, we'd better get moving soon or call Wish Dudek to move back the reservation."

Michelle dismissed them, and Liza humped her walker down the hallway to reception, where she exchanged goodbyes with Ysabel. Then she and Michael got on the elevator.

As they rode down, Liza glanced over at Michael. "You were very quiet in there."

"Liza, I love you dearly," he told her, "but I've learned from hard experience not to stand between you and Michelle Markson—especially when Michelle is in a bad mood."

She examined his expression closely. "That's not the only reason."

He sighed. "It's one of the things you said in there, about running out of suspects. I wonder if that means the cops are, too—if they were even looking at any others."

Much as Liza would have liked to reassure Michael, she just didn't have anything to say. Every time they had managed to come up with a potential alternative suspect, he or she had been cleared.

"The cops have no hard evidence linking Lolly to what happened," she offered. "At best, they can try to make a circumstantial case. And," she added, "they have no motive."

"But Ritz sent her those puzzles, the same as she did with Sam Pang, who does have a motive," Michael said heavily.

"Maybe Ritz didn't have anything on Lolly," Liza suggested. "When Darrie Brunswick offered Lolly the Boots Bungalow, Ritz made a big deal about sharing it with her. They didn't really move in the same circles. It's possible that Ritz wanted to get close in hopes of digging up something she could use for blackmail."

"God help us—and Lolly—if Ritz found anything." Michael broke off as the elevator doors opened on the downstairs lobby. "It would be all too easy to imagine Ritz opening her nasty mouth in the bungalow right before the quake."

He went to get the door, and Liza followed in silence. She'd been thinking the exact same thing.

In spite of L.A.'s snarled traffic patterns, they made it to the restaurant in the Valley well on time. It was a rustic sort of operation in a Spanish colonial building whose plaster walls and roof tiles had become weathered but not grubby—a mellow place, especially the outdoor courtyard where Wish sat at an umbrella-shaded table, enjoying a glass of wine.

With the authority of a long-standing regular, Wish recommended the Cobb salad. Michael and Liza fell in with the suggestion, Michael adding a bottle of beer and Liza discovering that the wine list also offered a nonalcoholic sparkling cider.

Her drink came in a long flute, and she took a sip, savoring the sweet yet crisp taste.

This should go well with the high-class rabbit food, she thought. *And keeping away from the alcohol will let me take a painkiller if I decide I need one.*

She feared that by the time this lunch was over, she might want a painkiller or two.

Wish had a good supply of small talk, and he shared it while they waited for their salads.

"I guess the grand muckety-mucks got a little worried after your misadventure on the set," he told Liza. "They've had people going over the entire soundstage with a fine-toothed comb making sure everything is sturdy—no hidden cracks, no chance the roof will fall in on us."

He took a sip of his wine. "And it looks as if we'll be back in regular production starting Monday. Celebrity Week will be postponed for a couple of months, until the memory of the quake fades a bit—and maybe this thing with Ritz is resolved."

"Speaking of the quake, I never got a chance to thank you—at least not while I was in my right mind—for your help that day."

Liza rose from her seat, took a couple of careful, tottery steps with one hand on the table, and leaned down to kiss Wish on the cheek.

"I would say that's reward enough," he said gallantly.

Michael jumped up to help Liza back to her seat. "That

was such a crazy scene." He shook his head. "People running around, screaming, mass confusion. One thing's for sure. I bet anyone who went through it will remember where he or she was at the moment of the quake."

Wish sat very still. "After what I heard on *The Lowdown* last night, I guess I should appreciate that you're the one asking the question, Michael."

He looked over at Liza. "Do you think I'm some sort of . . . suspect?" A few extra lines seemed to appear around his eyes.

Liza decided to put her cards on the table. "Do you like Lolly Popovic?" she asked.

"That depends how you define the word 'like,'" Wish replied cautiously. "She's a nice kid—although at my age anybody under forty has now become a kid. Her mom was a babe among babes in my younger days."

"In this case, I'm asking if you like Lolly enough to try and help her avoid a trial and maybe prison," Liza said.

"I hope you're not talking perjury." Wish picked up his glass. "It's a little late for me to suddenly say that Lolly and I were having lunch. I already told the cops the true story."

"Nothing so dramatic," Michael assured him. "I assume you know what happened to Lolly—she took a knock on the head—"

"I've been hearing things about amnesia," Wish interrupted. "So she doesn't know where she was—or what she did."

Michael nodded. "It leaves her open to a very raw deal from the cops."

"I'd like to help," Wish said, "but I didn't see her after she left the studio with Ritz Tarleton."

"We know that Ritz put pressure on several of the contestants to lose the first game—the one that was taped," Liza told him. "That gives us some people with motive. She was also insulting to a lot of the people on the set—"

"Including me," Wish admitted. "I'd hear comments like

'old man' or 'has-been' in her voice behind my back." He shrugged. "Frankly, I wondered if she was nerving herself to say them to my face."

"You sound a lot less"—Liza fumbled for a word—"*sensitive* about it than Darrie."

"Darrie's reached a point in her life—well, let's be frank. Actresses her age don't get much work. She's always complaining to me that guys in the Business get distinguished—women get old."

He shrugged. "I, on the other hand—I think I'm old. I use words that most people don't anymore. Like 'actress'—nowadays they're female actors, aren't they?"

"I think it's just plain 'actors,'" Michael said.

Wish spread his hands in an "I give up" gesture. "Instead of a stereo or home entertainment system, or even a record player, I call it a Victrola. That's what my folks called it when I was growing up, and it sticks in my head."

He looked from Liza to Michael with a quizzical expression. "I'm not ready to retire next month. I've got a contract for three more seasons and hope to work for more, God willing. But I've done a whole lot of stuff. Had my chances—the talk show didn't pan out." Wish tilted his head to one side with a wry smile. Then he straightened up, getting serious. "But I've put in twenty-five solid years making *D-Kodas* a top syndication franchise. That's a pretty good career for a guy who started out as the funny weatherman on a local newscast."

His smile quirked a little farther into self-mockery. "Guess I'm right behind Letterman at the top of that list."

"So what did you do after the director called a lunch break?" Liza asked.

"First and foremost, I got out of there," Wish replied. "No sense hanging around when Darrie gets in a loud mood like that. I went to my dressing room, debating whether I should hit the studio commissary or clean off my makeup and go out for lunch."

He shook the table a little. "Then the whole joint began to move. I got outdoors as quickly as possible. Found a bunch of stagehands milling around and organized them to try and do something helpful."

Wish gave them a snappy salute. "I was a corporal in the army a long, long time ago. Guess the instinct doesn't die off. Anyway, we cleared away a little debris, helped a couple of injured people—" He looked at Liza. "And then I found you."

She nodded. "And the rest is history."

Looks as if Wish has a pretty good alibi, Liza thought. *He might have been alone at the first shock, but he had people around him right after he stepped out of the soundstage.*

"How about Darrie?" Michael asked hopefully.

Wish shook his head. "She had someone with her from the moment she stormed off the set. The line producer was in her dressing room, trying to calm her down—not very successfully, judging from the noise level coming through the wall. The executive producer arrived just in time for the quake. He hustled Darrie off to wherever they keep the valuable studio properties."

"Is that what they did with the celebrity contestants?" Liza asked.

"I think things were a little too disorganized to do that," Wish replied. "At least at first. I saw Claudio Day and that hip-hop character in the crowd I pulled the stagehands out of. Claudio joined us to help out for a while, but one of the production flunkies came and led him away. I assume the same happened with the other guy."

"How about Sam Pang?" Michael asked a little desperately.

But Wish just shook his head. "Didn't see her at all. I got the impression she wouldn't be much help in an emergency." He speared a chunk of avocado on his fork. "Sorry if I can't be more helpful."

"Yeah, well, I'm sorry this turned out to be a less than convivial lunch," Liza apologized.

They finished the meal in glum silence. Neither Liza nor Michael was in the mood to discuss what they'd just heard, and Wish had apparently run out of small talk.

In the car on the way home, though, Michael spoke up. "We've still got Sam Pang and Chard Switzer to account for."

"Chard was the most forthcoming of the people we questioned," Liza pointed out. "And Sam was pretty up-front about the blackmail."

"Maybe there's another motive we're not seeing," Michael suggested. "Did Fritz Tarleton have any dealings in Korea? Maybe he screwed over Sam's family back home."

"Or maybe Ritz had a tempestuous affair with the third assistant lighting tech." Liza let her sarcasm hang right out there. "Who happened to be psychic, so he knew an earth-quake was coming to hide traces of his murder."

"If he was psychic, he should have known the affair would end badly," Michael joked, joining in the game with his best script-doctor style. "Besides, it's unlikely. We already established that Ritz wouldn't sleep with writers, so I think that eliminates lighting techs as well."

Liza looked over at him from her seat. "What, are you miffed?"

"Relieved, actually," Michael admitted. "Otherwise Ritz would have made a play for me just to annoy you— and that would land me on Quigley's suspect list."

"Not to mention my S-list," Liza responded, and then stopped for a beat. "Uh, I mean, she's just a nasty piece of work. You'd go down in everyone's estimation if they saw her hanging off you."

He glanced at her from behind the driver's wheel. "Of course. Yeah. Okay."

They drove the rest of the way in pensive silence.

Why did the thought of Ritz and Michael together get such a rise out of me? Liza worried. *Don't we have enough on our minds?*

They went into the house, and Michael monitored the

voice mail again, zipping past any unfamiliar phone numbers. "Either media or gossip rag calls," he said.

Then he stopped at one call, letting it play through.

"Liza, it's Elise Halvorsen. Haven't heard from you lately, so I thought I'd give you a call." Meticulous as ever, she left her phone number and said good-bye to the machine.

A huge wave of guilt washed over Liza. "It's almost a week. I stuck her with Rusty for longer than I intended—and a lot longer than she'd appreciate. He's probably overturned her sofa or something."

"You don't know that sofa," Michael told her. "The upholstery may be mushy, but the damned thing weighs a ton."

"You don't know Rusty," Liza replied grimly as she punched in the Maiden's Bay number.

Mrs. Halvorsen answered on the third ring.

"Hi, Mrs. H. I'm so sorry I haven't spoken to you," Liza apologized into the handset. "It's just been crazy here."

"I know," her neighbor replied. "I've seen you a couple of times on TV. You really should get some tennis balls to put on the legs of that walker. Friends of mine say they make it a lot easier to move that thing around."

"I'll look into that when I get home," Liza promised. "Which should be fairly soon. They've decided to put off the whole celebrity thing a few months, and who knows what they'll do when that time finally rolls around? They may go with an entirely different theme."

"You mean, considering how tragically it all turned out?" Mrs. H.'s voice took on an eager lilt. "If you're coming home soon, does that mean you've solved the murder?"

If I had and told you, it would be all over Maiden's Bay before suppertime, Liza thought.

Aloud, she said, "Not yet, I'm afraid," shifting a nervous glance over to Michael.

"Tell her I said hello," he mouthed.

"Michael says hello," Liza obediently added. "And I hope Rusty hasn't been making a nuisance of himself."

"You're classing me in with the nuisances now?" Michael burst out.

Liza hushed him, trying to listen to her neighbor.

"Well, he almost took a bite out of my nice widower friend Ed," Mrs. Halvorsen admitted.

Liza almost dropped the phone in shock. *"What?"*

"I guess Rusty thought we were wrestling." Mrs. H. started to giggle. "Haven't had anything like that happen since my courting days."

TMI, Liza thought, literally speechless. An odd ringtone filled the silence.

"Speak of the devil," Mrs. H. said. "He's texting me."

She sighed. "I wish he'd just call. Texting him back is such a chore. The keys are so small."

"I know how that feels." Liza thought of Michael's miniature laptop. What was it with men sometimes?

"I learned to type on an old Remington manual," Mrs. H. said. "The keys were stiff enough to break your fingernails, but at least the keyboard was big enough to accommodate two hands."

Liza heard her neighbor's nails click against the little phone—missing the key, apparently. "I'm still not used to working on only nine little buttons," Mrs. H. complained. "How do I say, 'Not now'? The *N* is on the sixth button, so I tap that two times . . ."

Liza's eye fell on one of the mystery puzzles Ritz had created. In the first subgrid, the sixth space had a two in it.

"Um, Mrs. H., something just came up," she said into the phone. "Can I give you a buzz back a little later? . . . Right. Thanks. Give Rusty a hug. Bye."

She hung up and turned to see Michael give her a reproachful look. "I know it might be trying to listen to the neighborhood gossip at long-distance rates, but that was a pretty ruthless way to cut Mrs. H. short. 'Something came up,' huh?"

"Something did." Liza pointed to the phone she'd just hung up. "What do you see?"

"A telephone."

"I mean on the face of it."

"Oh—the keypad?"

Liza picked up one of the puzzle sheets and used it to cover the bottom row of keys—the *, 0, and #. "Now what do you see?"

"Three-quarters of the keypad?" Michael offered blankly.

"How about a nine-space array, just like a sudoku sub-grid," Liza said. "Nine—actually eight keys that, if you tap them one to four times, can encode a text message with all twenty-six letters."

She tapped the phone's keys. "A code key that sits in everyone's home and in a lot of people's pockets nowadays—and maybe the key to Ritz Tarleton's puzzle messages."

15

Leaning over the side of the sofa, Liza placed the telephone front and center on the end table.

"You'd better bring another chair over here," she told Michael.

"I'm not going to lug any of these armchairs." Instead, he went into the dining room and returned with a chair from the set there, placing it right in front of the table.

Meanwhile, Liza gathered up the puzzles Ritz had sent to Sam Pang and Lolly Popovic. "When we were trying this before, we wondered if there were clues we should skip. So now I'll only be looking for ones, twos, threes, and maybe fours. I'll give the space and the number in it, and you'll use the keypad to say what letter that's supposed to be."

"Okay," Michael said. "Fire away."

Liza picked up the puzzle she'd glanced at while talking on the phone. "This is the one that gave me the idea. Mrs. H. was sending a text message from her cell phone and mentioned that she was tapping twice on the sixth key. I noticed that the sixth space in the first subgrid on the puzzle had a two."

"So the first letter is *N*," Michael said.

"Right," Liza said, writing it down. "The next of our target numbers is right next door, in space four of the second grid. It's a three."

	7					9	3	2
		2	3	5				
			7		9			
		3		1				9
	4		8		5			
	5			7			8	
	3	9			2	8	4	
			8			7		
		6						

"Box four, three, third letter . . . That's an *I*," Michael reported.

Liza added that and moved on. "Third subgrid, space two, showing another three."

Michael peered at the keypad. "The third letter there is *C*."

"Uh-huh." Liza's pen scratched away at the bottom of the paper. "Now, right beside it, third subgrid again, third space, but this time there's a two."

"Second letter? That's an *E*."

Liza added it. "Well, at least that gives us a word—nice."

"Don't get too enthusiastic," Michael warned her. "We got words before—they just didn't make any sense together."

Liza was already looking ahead on the puzzle. "Well, there are only four more clues that we'd be interested in, so let's see."

She put her finger down on the side of the puzzle. "Fourth subgrid, third space again."

"Okay . . ."

"This time it's a three instead of a two."

"And this time it's an *F* instead of an *E*," Michael said.

Liza added the new letter to the bottom of the page. "Fifth subgrid, second space, and we've got a one."

"Makes sense. That's the first letter of the alphabet—*A*," Michael told her.

Her pen scratched that letter in. "Subgrid seven, second space again, this time a three," Liza read off. "Did we do this before?"

"Yes," Michael told her. "It was a *C*."

She added that, then read, "Eighth subgrid, third space, number two—we've done that one, too."

Michael nodded. "It's an *E* again."

She handed him the paper, and he read the two words at the bottom. "Nice face."

"Considering what Ritz did to Samantha, I'd say that makes a definite connection," Liza said. "I was there to catch her reaction when she saw her face in the mirror. She was pretty much creeped out just getting sudoku from Ritz. Imagine how she'd feel discovering a message like this in the puzzle."

"Imagination may be all we have here," Michael told her with a dubious frown. "Apply this 'code key' to any hundred sudoku, and I bet at least one of them will yield some kind of message that would seem relevant."

"Well, 'nice face' seems a hell of a lot more relevant than 'love her globes,'" Liza retorted. "Let's be scientific about this and try to decode the other puzzle that went to Sam."

"The one with the errors in it," Michael said.

Liza nodded. "The one that Uncle Jim thought more likely to have a message embedded."

"When you told me about your IM chat, your uncle wasn't so positive," Michael argued. "He said something like the errors made it possible that there was a message."

Liza picked up the sheet with the second puzzle on it. "Let's stop talking and see what's likely or possible."

She started reading off the relevant clues. "First subgrid, a one in the sixth space."

"That's an *M*."

"Same subgrid, a three in the ninth space."

"That's a *Y*."

"So we have an M-Y already," she told Michael triumphantly.

He gave her a dubious frown. "And if we do three more, we might end up with something like M-Y-Z-R-Q."

"Okay, we'll keep going and see. Moving on to the second subgrid, we have a three in the third space. We've seen that already." She screwed up her face, trying to remember. "Is that an *E*?"

"No, it's an *F*."

She wrote that down and moved on. "Third subgrid, sixth space—a three."

"That's an *O*."

Noting that, Liza scanned farther along in the puzzle.

				5	3		4	
	5	1		7				3
		3	8				7	
6			7			9		2
	4		9		2	5		8
9		8		6				
	7			8	6			
	3				3		3	4
8	9		5			6		

"Fifth subgrid, sixth space, we have a two—that's an *N*, right?"

Michael nodded. "Which so far gives us M-Y-F-O-N— and more a jumbled collection of letters than a message."

Liza felt her own niggle of doubt but doggedly went on. "Sixth subgrid, third space, two. Wait a minute, I remember this one—*E*."

"That's right." Michael sounded a bit smug. "Doesn't seem to be getting any clearer, does it?"

Liza's only response was to move on in the puzzle. "Seventh subgrid—the lower left-hand corner. There's a three in the fifth space."

"The middle square." Michael looked at the keypad. "That's an *L*."

"Eighth subgrid, another three in the sixth space."

"Which gets us an *O*," Michael said.

"And finally, another three in the middle space in the last subgrid, which is an *L*," Liza finished.

Michael snatched the paper. "Which gives us— M-Y-F-O-N-E-L-O-L. Looks pretty much random to me."

Liza frowned, took the paper back, and said, "Not necessarily." After making two slashes with her pen, she handed the puzzle to Michael again.

"MY/FONE/LOL," he read. "So you're saying Ritz couldn't spell?"

"I'm saying that people who text simplify their messages—otherwise their thumbs would fall off. 'L-O-L' is texting shorthand for 'laugh out loud.' And 'F-O-N-E' is quicker to type than 'P-H-O-N-E.' Ritz did have a picture of Sam Pang's 'nice face' on her phone. The fact that the 'LOL' she added at the end invalidates the puzzle just sort of rubs it in."

"A brilliant theory, ably argued," Michael told her. "But I'm still not convinced."

"On to Lolly's messages." Liza got that sheet and began. "First subgrid, eighth space, there's a two."

"Which turns out to be a *U*."

"We move to the subgrid next door, seventh space, a three."

"That's an *R*."

"And up and over in the same grid is a two in the sixth space—that's an *N*." Liza marked it down.

"Giving us U-R-N. So either it's a big pot, or Lolly has to earn, as in make money, to pay blackmail." Michael tried to keep his voice light, but Liza could see he was beginning to get tired of this. She hurried on. "Third subgrid, second space with a one—that's an *A*, right?"

"Yup," Michael said.

"And then right below it is a three in the fifth space."

"Which is an *L*." He craned his neck to check the letters that Liza had written down. "Aha! Maybe Ritz misspelled 'urinal.'"

Liza didn't rise to the bait, choosing to go on. "We skip

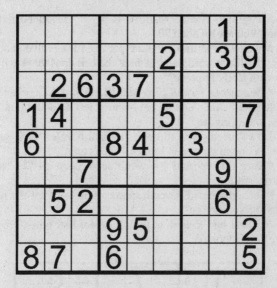

the next two subgrids, apparently because it would put con-flicting clues on the same line. The sixth grid has a three in the fourth space."

"That's an *I*."

"Then comes a two in the third space of the next grid. I'm starting to get the hang of this—it's an *E*, right?"

"Right," Michael agreed.

"And finally, a two in the sixth space of the last grid—moved over to keep the same clue from appearing in one column, and yielding an *N*."

"Which gives us U-R-N-A-L-I-E-N, which sounds like some sort of synthetic fabric." Michael sounded trium-phant. "Or do you think Ritz is warning Lolly about tax problems and saying she should 'earn a lien'?"

Liza looked at the letters for a long moment, then began to smile. "I think there's some more texting shorthand going on here. Sound out the first three letters."

Shrugging, Michael read, "U-R-N . . ." He looked at the rest. "You are an alien?"

Michael burst into laughter, patting Liza on the shoulder. "Brilliant wordplay, but what the hell does that have to do with Lolly Popovic?"

"There's one more," Liza said. "Let's just do it, okay?"

Michael said, "Okay," but his tone left no doubt that he was humoring her.

Liza started going through the final puzzle. "First subgrid, a one in the second space—that's an *A*."

"Keep this up, and you won't need me at all," he said with a smile.

"Second subgrid, seventh space, a four—we haven't had one of those before."

Michael had to look at the phone for that one. "That's an *S*," he reported.

	1			7		4	6	
6				8			2	5
8			4		6		7	
5						6	8	
	4			5				1
9		3	3					
		8					9	
	6	3			1		5	4
	5		8		7			

"Next grid, we've got a two in the fifth space."

He had to consult the keypad again. "That's a *K*."

She looked at him. "Should I point out now that we have 'ask'?"

"As you said, let's keep going."

Liza went back to scanning the puzzle. "Fourth subgrid, a three in the last space."

"Third letter under nine." Michael peered at the key. "That's a *Y*. And maybe I should get one of those big-button phones in here."

"Or reading glasses," Liza needled him. "Moving to the next grid, we have a three in the seventh space. That's an *R*?"

"Right you are," Michael agreed.

"Then in the sixth subgrid, there's a one in the sixth space."

"That gives you an *M*," Michael reported after a glance at the phone.

In the seventh subgrid, the sixth space has a three. A one there meant *M*, so a three is *O*?"

"You got it," Michael said.

The next and last clue was in the eighth subgrid. "A one in the sixth space—that's an *M* again," Liza said.

She and Michael looked in silence at the line of letters, which seemed to break naturally into "ASK YR MOM."

" 'Ask your mom.' Well, that's weird," Michael finally said. "Not necessarily convincing, but definitely weird."

"Four puzzles yielding four messages?" Liza asked.

"If you define 'message' as a group of words created by arbitrarily twisting a collection of letters," he replied.

" 'Nice face' and 'my phone' pretty well fit in with what happened to Samantha Pang," Liza argued.

"But 'you're an alien' and 'ask your mom' don't seem to fit anything that happened to Lolly," Michael shot back. "Unless you figure Ritz intended to drug Lolly and make her up as a Klingon."

"Then there's the pattern in the way the puzzles were delivered," Liza pressed on. "The first seems reasonable enough, if a little cluttered—it looks as if Ritz is trying to help. But the next one has an obvious error—a deliberate error."

She pointed to the sudoku in question. "She didn't have to put the LOL in the message. It forces her to put three threes in a row across the bottom of the puzzle. And the 'ask your mom' puzzle—there was plenty of room left to arrange the last two letter-bearing clues so that they didn't conflict. Instead, she deliberately put the *O* in 'mom' under the *Y* in 'YR'—two threes in the same column."

"Two occurrences do not necessarily make a pattern."

"I'd say two occurrences are the minimum necessary for a pattern," Liza retorted.

"I might be willing to concede that it's a bit too much for coincidence that the puzzles for Sam Pang mention her face and a phone." Michael shrugged and then shook his head.

"But even granting that the words we dug out of Lolly's puzzles are a message, what do they mean? Lolly should ask her mom about being an alien? Her mom was abducted by aliens and impregnated with their probes?" He laughed. "I'm sure the tabloids would have had a field day if Rikki had even hinted at that."

Liza laughed, too—but at him. "Sometimes you are such a science-fiction nerd. Rikki *is* an alien—a resident alien with a green card."

"Well, yeah, but—"

But Liza wasn't listening any longer. She dug out her wallet, looking through the pockets for a card she'd been given.

"What are you doing?" Michael asked as she scooted back over to the phone.

"Calling Fritz Tarleton." She cut off the rest of her reply

because someone picked up the phone on the tour tycoon's private line.

"Tarleton here." Fritz Tarleton's voice was unmistakable.

"I sort of expected to get a secretary," Liza said into the phone. "Oh, sorry. This is—"

"Ms. Kelly," Tarleton finished for her. "I'm not sure whether I should be glad or worried that you've called."

"I'm trying to track down some information from when you tried to get Ritz interested in the family business. When she was working for you, did she have an office and a telephone?"

"Of course," he replied.

"Could you check the long-distance records? I need to know if she was talking to anyone in Mexico."

"I'd be surprised if she didn't," Tarleton said. "We have a lot of contacts down there. When we were doing the show, Ritz did a string of episodes about Cabo San Lucas."

He promised to get on it right away. Liza thanked him and hung up—to find Michael looming over her.

"Now that you're off the phone, can you explain what's going on here? What's this stuff about Ritz talking to people in Mexico?"

She nodded—not happily. "It has to do with a romantic story Lolly told me over hamburgers."

"When did you—Oh, right, when I was ferrying Rikki around after we met on the pier." He sat down beside her on the couch. "So, romance and hamburgers?"

"While we ate, Lolly told me how her mother and father were married on Lukas Popovic's boat—while they were sailing around the Sea of Cortez."

"Also known as the Gulf of California," Michael said.

"Mr. Tarleton just told me that Ritz spent some time taping episodes of their tour show at Cabo San Lucas."

"Which is in Baja California." Michael nodded his comprehension. "But I still don't see—"

Before he could say more, the ringing phone interrupted him. Liza picked it up.

"Ms. Kelly? Fritz Tarleton here."

Liza had to keep herself from looking at the phone in awe. "I didn't expect—"

"One nice thing about being the boss. When you ask, things get done quickly," Tarleton said. "The records show that Ritz called a lot of friends in Europe, South America, and even Japan." He sighed. "I suspect there was a lot of money wasted on those bills. But she also called Mike—Miguel—Obregon in Mexico."

"Do you know this Obregon?" Liza asked.

"We used to call him the Mayor of Baja," Tarleton said reminiscently. "He was a local fixer who freelanced doing . . . I guess you'd call them lucrative favors for well-off tourists. I was the first to see how useful it would be to have him working in our organization."

No time for war stories, Liza thought. "So you and Ritz both knew him?" she asked.

"He set up most of our shooting down in Cabo," Tarleton replied. "That was some years ago. He's pretty much retired now."

"But Ritz still had his number," Liza said. "Could I get that, please?"

Tarleton gave her a number with a 52 country code in front. "I'm not sure how this could tie in to what happened to Ritz." A bit of his tycoon-to-subordinate persona came over the line.

"I'm not sure if it does," Liza told him. "But I hope to know after I talk with Mr. Obregon."

They hung up again, and Liza punched in the number she'd copied down.

"Bueno," a male voice answered on the other end.

"Um, Mr.—uh, Señor Obregon? My name is Liza Kelly—"

"Then this must be about what happened to poor Ritz." The voice switched over to fluent English.

"Yes, it is," Liza said slowly. "Did Mr. Tarleton just call you?"

"No, but I keep seeing your name and picture next to her every time I watch *The Lowdown*," Obregon replied.

"I didn't know that they'd penetrated the Mexican market."

"I get it on my satellite dish," the Mexican said dryly. "So how can I help you? Ritz was a friend."

"Her father gave me this number after I asked him to check if she'd been speaking with anyone in Mexico."

"It was some months ago," Obregon told her. "She was supposed to be working in Fritz's office, and I thought she was just bored. She asked about a story I told her years ago when they were shooting down at Cabo."

"And what was that story, Mr. Obregon?"

"Mike," he corrected her. "It goes back even more years past, when people were just beginning to discover Baja. This rich American came to me, saying he needed a wedding—or something like it—as soon as possible."

"So you arranged the wedding?"

"Something like it," Obregon obliquely replied. "The Church requires banns to be announced and so on, and even the *alcalde*'s office would have held things up with paperwork. But I had a friend—a bartender—who did amateur theatricals and had a monk's robe, and I found a nice parchment with impressive-looking seals. It might have been a deed; it's so long ago now I don't really remember. I put on my good suit and pretended to be the mayor, and my bartender friend officiated over the vows on the American's yacht."

"A sailboat?" Liza asked.

"Yes," Obregon said. "He was very generous in his thanks. I sometimes wondered what happened to them. That's probably why I mentioned it to Ritz."

I think I know what happened, Liza thought uncomfortably. "One more question, even though you may find it silly. Do you have a big black mustache?"

Mike Obregon laughed heartily. "No."

But as Liza let go a sigh of relief, he said, "I'm afraid it's all gone white now."

16

Liza returned the telephone handset to the receiver with a sick feeling.

Just keep it inside—don't let on, she told herself. *There's no need to get Michael upset.*

But he was right beside her, looking at her closely. "I don't know what any of that was about," he told her. "But from the look on your face, it has to be bad news."

So much for that hope.

"I was talking with Mike Obregon, a guy who worked for Tarleton Tours down in Baja. Before that, he was sort of a freelance arranger, providing expensive services for foreign tourists."

"So?" Michael said a little impatiently.

"He helped set things up when Tarleton's tourism show shot some episodes down in Cabo. And apparently he told Ritz an old war story that she connected with Lolly Popovic. It's sort of the flip side to Lolly's romantic wedding tale." Liza took a breath. "The dark side."

"Liza, you're trying so hard to soften the blow that you're confusing me," Michael told her. "Just spit it out, okay?"

"Lukas Popovic hired Obregon to arrange a phony wedding for Rikki," Liza said. "It wasn't legally sanctioned in Mexico, and it wasn't even officiated by a real priest. She wound up with a fancy parchment in Spanish that he thinks was a property deed."

Michael sat in silence for a moment, shaking his head. "Back in the day, Lukas Popovic was known to have a pretty strange sense of humor."

"I think they always say that about directors," Liza said.

"You're just saying that because the last one you tangled with was a bit of a sadist." Michael went back to his story. "Anyway, Popovic loved to pull pranks on the set, the more expensive, the better. Maybe this one was a joke he couldn't take back."

Liza preferred to take a less charitable view. "Or maybe it was a way to shut Rikki up if she'd been bugging him to marry her. It doesn't matter now. He's dead and can't explain himself."

Michael nodded. "But it does leave a problem for Lolly. She may really be an alien—an illegal alien."

"That's probably pushing it," Liza said. "But she definitely has problems with her immigration status."

Michael laughed—a little grimly. "I guess once a publicist, always a publicist. You don't need to sugarcoat the situation. It's just us here."

"At this point, I wish I was a lawyer," Liza replied. "I'm not sure of the legalities. If Lukas Popovic was a naturalized citizen—"

"You mean if he didn't fake that, too," Michael put in. "We're talking twenty years ago. Things were a bit less crazy on the immigration issue back then."

"If Lolly's dad was a citizen—" Liza started again.

"Oh, the whole 'anchor baby' thing," Michael said. "She'd really be legal. So why are you looking at me with such a funny expression?"

"Besides not being able to get a word in edgewise?" Liza

asked. "I guess it's the publicist in me. Lolly would have to jump through a bunch of legal hoops—proving that Lukas was her father, for instance. If the tabloids got a whiff of this, they'd have a field day."

"I hadn't thought of that," Michael admitted. "Lolly always came across as the All-American Girl. How would people react if they discovered that title had been outsourced?"

He laughed, but Liza didn't.

"I think we just discovered why Ritz just about broke her neck to get on *D-Kodas* . . . and the scam that she hoped to pull on the set."

Michael's sense of plot took over. "She wanted to get next to Lolly because of that film deal."

"Stanley Lumiere is one of the greatest directors alive today," Liza said. "Even if the film doesn't make bazillions, it's sure to be a critical success. Chard Switzer was hoping to make a good impression on Lolly so she'd put in a good word for him with Lumiere."

"And Ritz wanted the same thing." Now Michael sounded as sick as Liza felt. "Except she had the ammunition to force Lolly to get her on the film."

He shook his head as if he were trying to get some kind of insect out of his ear. "Ritz Tarleton in a Stanley Lumiere production. The mind boggles."

"From what I hear, Lumiere is kind of a quirky guy," Liza said. "If Ritz got an audition and gave as good a performance as she gave scamming people . . ."

"Yeah, that's the upside, if things went perfectly." Michael's face fell into a dark scowl. "But if she didn't get the part—or the audition—well, Ritz was desperate, wasn't she? She wouldn't hesitate to ruin Lolly's life."

Liza looked at Michael as he took the facts to their logical conclusion. "Dammitall, Liza, we just turned up a grade-A, number-one motive for Lolly Popovic to kill Ritz Tarleton."

He shot up from the sofa and began pacing around the living room. "This is all that Quigley and the celebrity squad need. They have opportunity—Lolly was the last person seen with Ritz before she died. You could even say they have means. That old bungalow was probably never brought up to the earthquake standards in the new building code. The place would have been a death trap in a serious tremor. Lolly has lived here all her life; she'd be earthquake-savvy. She'd know that one push could shut Ritz up forever."

"And now they'd have motive," Liza said in a tight voice. "If Ritz decided to make her pitch while they were alone in the bungalow and the ground began to shake, Lolly could have thrown her back into the collapsing building."

"Could she really do that?" Michael asked, grasping desperately for any reason to disbelieve the scenario they were building. "The girls were both the same size, and Lolly isn't built like you—"

He broke off, realizing the mental minefield he'd just wandered into. "I mean, she's one of those skinny minnies who look good on camera."

"Nice footwork, Langley," she complimented him ironically.

"I'm just saying, did she have the muscle to throw Ritz all that distance?"

"You're acting as if it were all premeditated," Liza said. "If the quake happened right after Ritz dropped her bomb and Lolly was just about crazy with anger . . ."

"Oh, you're talking that whole hysterical-strength thing." Michael unconsciously flexed his arm muscles. "Sort of like turning into the Incredible Hulk without going green."

"I never liked the idea of calling it 'hysterical,'" Liza complained. "But there are cases of people in extreme states showing tremendous physical ability. Parents single-handedly lifting cars to save their children, that kind of thing."

Michael nodded. "Okay, so Lolly flew into a rage and then sent Ritz flying. It's possible, and Quigley is sure to buy it. The big question is, if it happened, does Lolly even remember it?"

"It complicates things," Liza said. "She now has a strong psychological reason to forget—not just blotting out the murder, but the memory of Ritz kicking her life to pieces right before."

Then she went on, because it had to be said. "And if she's faking, well, it's acting of the kind of caliber that deserves to be in a Stanley Lumiere film."

Her legs twitched. She wished she could be up and pacing, too.

"There's another thing." Liza looked up at Michael, pleading for him to understand. "We can't sit on this. Quigley has already been all over us for hindering his investigation. We've argued that any information we come across is stuff he already knows or could easily uncover. But the puzzles—the code—these are things he'd never find out."

She stared at his face, reading his features. It was one thing to come up with a theory, even to entertain suspicions in private. But talking to Quigley would mean putting someone in danger of a murder prosecution—a friend's child.

"We barely know Lolly." His voice was hoarse, barely above a whisper. "Met her—what? Two, three times? But I liked her. What do you think, Liza? You spent more time with her."

"Over hamburgers," Liza tried to dodge.

"You take a longer time to make your mind up about people than I do. I might have been taken in by her PR. You wouldn't. So what do you think, Liza?"

"I liked her, too," Liza admitted. "She seemed like a talented kid, ambitious, but not snotty about it. And she seemed genuinely upset about her memory loss."

But she's an actor, Liza went on silently. She could have been channeling shock over killing Ritz into a performance of amnesia.

She didn't want to say that to Michael. Looking into his eyes, though, she could see he was thinking the same thing.

"Okay. We'll call Quigley. But—but not yet," he said. "I've got to call Rikki first. Whatever Lolly knows—or doesn't know—this is going to rock Rikki's world. She deserves a little time to get ready."

He went to the phone and got directory assistance, asking for the number of the motel where they'd left the Popovics.

"I hope they're still there," Liza said.

Michael got the front office and asked if Edna Stepanek was registered. "Rikki usually uses her mother's maiden name," he explained, his hand over the receiver.

He took his hand away. "Yes? Good. Thank you."

A moment later he said, "Rikki? It's Michael Langley. I think you'd better sit down. I've got some bad news. Those puzzles that Ritz gave to Lolly, they had messages— threats, really—coded into them. Ritz worked in Mexico a while ago—yes, Mexico. Somebody told her a story—"

He broke off. "There's no easy way to say this. Lukas arranged a fake wedding when you were down there, this guy was involved with it, and Ritz got the story. We know she wasn't above blackmail . . . so this will give the cops motive."

Michael shook his head. "I can't do that, Rikki. We have to tell the police. But I wanted you to know first. You'll have to get things ready. Yes, more doctors." He glanced at Liza. "We'll get you the best lawyer—yes, yes, I guess the two of you will have to talk for a bit. Okay. Call me back."

He hung up. "She asked if she could call Quigley, after she discusses things with Lolly. And then she'll call us to give in our evidence."

Liza looked at him. "I hope she's not just buying time so she and Lolly can make a run for Mexico."

"What good would that do?" Michael asked bitterly. "Lolly doesn't have a passport."

They sat in depressed silence for a while, until a strange noise came out of Michael's pocket.

"Text message," he said, pulling out his cell phone. But when he opened it and looked at the screen, he frowned. "It's from Lolly. She says she's waiting for me on the Santa Monica Pier, that I should come alone . . . that we need to talk."

Liza reached for her walker. "I'm coming, too."

Michael grabbed hold of the walker, shaking his head. "You've got a bad history with murderers—even potential murderers. They keep pointing guns at you."

He rattled the walker. "And with this thing, you won't even be able to duck."

Liza tried to argue, but Michael was adamant.

"All right," she finally said. "Call me on my cell when you get there. Leave the phone on. That way I'll be able to hear what's going on, and if you need backup."

He spread his hands in a placating gesture. "Okay, okay. I'm going now."

Liza shifted her grip from the walker to his arm, pulling him down and kissing him. "Be careful."

"That's my middle name," he assured her. Then he was out the door.

By the time she struggled to the window, the car had pulled down the driveway.

Liza returned to the couch, brooding. The living room she'd always thought of as cozy seemed downright tiny, the walls pressing in on her. She kept looking at her watch, but the hands refused to move.

Hell of a time for the battery to go dead, she thought, tapping the crystal.

Then the doorbell rang.

Liza shot to her feet, wincing at the painful protest from her injured knee. Grabbing the walker, she made her way to the door.

A pale-faced Rikki Popovic stood facing her. "Is Lolly here?"

"Um—n-no. She's not with you?"

Rikki only looked more upset. "She stepped out of our

room while I was talking with Michael. I thought she was just giving me privacy—" She paused. "But now I realize it was after I mentioned the word 'Mexico.' I thought she might come here."

"She sent Michael a text message to meet her at the Santa Monica Pier."

Rikki's shoulders slumped. "Thank God. I kept calling her cell, but she didn't answer. Lolly keeps telling me how impressed she was by him—and by you. Maybe we can call him in a little bit, ask him to bring her here . . ."

She wobbled a little in the doorway.

"Come in, come in." Liza brought the walker back.

I'm going to be useless if she faints, she thought.

Rikki closed the door, shaking her head. "It's just—I haven't eaten anything today."

"Follow me to the kitchen," Liza said. "We'll get some tea and toast into you."

The kitchen was not walker-friendly. It was also something of a mess—they hadn't cleaned up after breakfast this morning. Michael had cut lengths off a baguette, halved them, and made cinnamon toast. The room still smelled of it—and the butter, sugar, cinnamon, and leftover bread were still spread across the counter. The knife Michael had used to slice up the bread lay among the ingredients as well.

"Excuse the disorder," Liza apologized as she came to a stop in front of the sink. Balancing on one leg, she snagged the kettle and brought it over to the tap to fill it.

Rikki stepped behind her, and all of a sudden, cold metal pressed against Liza's neck.

"Now be quiet and do what I tell you," Rikki said.

17

Well, at least it's not a gun, Liza thought as she stood very still.

The knife at her throat was an undistinguished piece of cutlery. It had been around since before Michael and Liza got married—it might even date back to Michael's college days.

Its wooden handle was worn from use, but the blade still held a good edge when it was sharpened.

Liza carried a smudged scar near the knuckle of her left index finger from the time the knife slipped while she was slicing limes—blood all over the place—

Not the best memory to hold on to at the moment, she told herself.

"Start moving into the dining room—slowly," Rikki ordered.

As if I could do it any other way, Liza thought, moving her walker.

The dining area was about the size of a postage stamp, the table set in its smallest configuration with four chairs around it. Rikki prodded Liza over to one of the end chairs, the ones with arms. "Sit there."

Liza sank onto the seat as Rikki kicked the walker away. Now she stood in front of Liza, knife at the ready in her right hand, a roll of duct tape in the other.

"Use this to tape your right wrist to the chair," Rikki told her.

Liza took the tape, watching the blade mere inches from her face. *If this were one of Michael's scripts, I'd just do a backflip and bash Rikki with the chair.*

Unfortunately, there didn't seem to be much in the way of movie magic in the air. And Liza didn't think she could manage the backflip with two good legs, much less one gimpy one.

Like it or not, she did as Rikki told her, making herself even more helpless. When Liza's right arm was immobilized on the chair arm, Rikki took the tape and did the same with the left.

Nowadays, all the crime-scene shows catch people because of fingerprints they left on the sticky side of the tape, Liza thought. *If I mentioned this to Rikki, maybe she'd take a step back from what she's doing.*

Looking at the woman wrapping Liza's wrist in tape, knife held pirate-fashion between her teeth, Liza decided that rational argument wouldn't get very far.

Still, she had to try. "So, unless Lolly is lying in wait for Michael at Santa Monica, I guess you're the person we were really looking for."

The tape roll dropped, and the knife blade flashed in front of her eyes. "Lolly had nothing to do with it!" Rikki shouted. "I'm trying to protect her."

She got her volume down and the knife away from Liza. "I had an audition for a TV role in one of the other sections of the studio and stopped by the bungalow, figuring I'd wait there and have lunch with Lolly. But she wasn't there, only that—that—"

"Ritz?" Liza supplied when Rikki couldn't come up with a bad enough name for the deceased.

"She laughed at me, telling me the story she'd heard from her friend down in Mexico."

Rikki was definitely angry, but she didn't have the same crazy glint in her eye she'd shown when Liza suggested Lolly was involved in the killing.

And Lolly told me she'd never gotten a passport. The thought swam up from her memory.

"But you already knew about Lukas and the make-believe wedding, didn't you?" she said.

Rikki nodded. "When Lolly was a little girl I was looking for the license—what I thought was the license—to get a passport for her. We had a Mexican housekeeper—"

Like about 99 percent of the people in L.A. who can afford one, Liza thought.

"She got very excited to discover that I owned a piece of land near her hometown," Rikki went on. "That's when I discovered the license was a sham—the whole marriage, too."

She used the wrist of her knife hand to push her hair back out of her face, tore off another length of tape, and began fastening Liza's right ankle to the front chair leg.

"Lukas was much older than I was—almost twenty years," Rikki said.

About the same difference in years as there is between us, Liza thought.

"We argued a lot on the boat. I told him I was getting off at the next port and walking back if I had to. Instead, he got a priest, or so I thought." She softened a little. "I think he felt bad about it. All through his next film, he talked about having another ceremony, a big one, bringing my parents over from Poland. But I was enormous with Lolly at the time. We agreed to wait until after she was born. But then Lukas went sailing and never came back."

"And a few years later, you discovered you'd never really been married."

Rikki smiled bitterly. "Yeah, the joke was even worse than people said. The dumb Polish actress not only slept with the writer; she let him fool her into believing she was married. Even worse, people were getting crazier over the whole immigration thing. I kept hoping it would die down, but it just got worse."

"So you kept it hidden," Liza said.

Rikki's face hardened and that fanatical gleam came back to her eye. "And then that bitch started mocking me— 'Imagine what will happen when it turns out that America's sweetheart is actually an illegal alien.' She bragged that she had connections at *The Lowdown* to smear the story all over the country."

Rikki was working on Liza's other ankle now, pulling the tape so tight, she threatened to cut off circulation to the foot.

"Then Ritz told you she wanted a part in Lolly's film."

"Imagine that talentless drone in a Stanley Lumiere production!" Rikki seethed. "She'd gotten everything else she wanted in her life, so she was willing to jeopardize my daughter's career because she wanted this. And she *laughed* about it!"

Her face twisted. "Well, she stopped laughing when the earthquake started. We both ran for the door, but I got there first. She went to push past me, but got caught on something. So I pushed her back—"

Liza found herself remembering what happened to Chick Benson when the paparazzo tried to block Rikki's path.

"I just wanted her to see what it felt like to come in second. I didn't expect the whole house to come down."

"But you didn't get help for Ritz, either," Liza pointed out.

"I thought it was a gift from God," Rikki replied simply. "I just got out of there, thinking that Lolly would be able to prove she was somewhere else. She often went out for walks. But she got hurt, there was the whole amnesia thing, and the police suspected her."

She rose to her feet, gripping the knife. "And then you and Michael got involved, trying to help. When Michael called, saying you were going to the police, I had to do something. Lolly was in the bathroom. I took her phone to send Michael away and came here."

Liza could feel her heart pounding in her chest, but she managed to keep her voice calm. "What are you going to do, Rikki?"

"I would die for my daughter," Rikki said. "If I thought it would do any good, I would confess to killing that slut. But then the rest of the story would come out."

And she's already killed once to keep that from happening, Liza thought.

"It will look like a home invasion." Rikki wasn't really talking to her, just thinking out loud. "You were taken first; Michael comes back and walks in on it. I'll take some jewelry; there must be a computer, whatever electronics I can find . . ."

At the mention of Michael, Liza turned toward the living room where her cell phone still sat on the couch.

Why doesn't he call? she wondered. *He was supposed to ring me up when he got to the pier. Did something happen to him? Did I do something stupid like leave it on silent mode?*

Or maybe it wasn't so stupid. *If he calls and the phone just buzzes in the other room, it will go to voice mail. Michael will know something's up.*

Taped securely to this damned chair, Liza could do nothing else but hope—and maybe pray a little bit.

"Rikki—" Liza began.

"You won't talk me out of it." To ensure that, Rikki slapped a length of duct tape over Liza's mouth. Then she stayed looming over Liza with the knife. The silence stretched until it frayed almost as badly as their nerves.

Rikki jumped, nearly nicking Liza, when the refrigerator started cycling in the kitchen.

Then they heard the front door open—and Michael's voice. "Liza, no one was there."

You idiot! Liza silently screamed at him. *Why didn't you call? You're going to get killed because you didn't call!*

His voice came nearer, sounding worried but still unsuspecting. "Liza? Where are you?"

Rikki pressed herself against the wall by the entrance from the living room, knife raised.

But Michael didn't come ambling in; he charged, going for Rikki's knife hand.

He almost got it.

At least he deflected Rikki's stab. Even so, Liza winced to see the blade angled across Michael's chest, cutting into the muscle near his armpit.

Michael staggered past Liza toward the kitchen. Rikki came after him, out of Liza's sight line. All she heard were the sounds of scuffling—then Rikki came tottering back, slashing wildly.

A second later, Michael followed, holding Liza's discarded walker.

For a few moments, it looked like some surreal version of geriatric lion taming, Michael fending off Rikki with the walker. But Liza watched in horror as the wet red blotch on his shirt got bigger and bigger.

Then Lolly Popovic appeared in the entranceway. "Mom, you've got to stop this!"

"Go away! Get out!" Rikki tried to angle herself so that her knife threatened Michael while her body hid the bloody blade from her daughter—an impossible geometry.

Lolly stepped between her mother and Michael. "I knew something was wrong when I came out of the bathroom and you were gone. Then I looked on my phone and found that message to Michael. I ran to the pier—caught him as he came in the parking area. When we didn't find you in Santa Monica, we rushed right here."

Lolly gulped for breath. "On the way, Michael told me about Mexico—what Ritz found out." She stared at her mother in horror. "I wouldn't believe what you did to her, till I saw this."

"It was for you!" The cry came torn from Rikki's throat.

"If you got her the part, do you think that would be the end of it? Ritz Tarleton was the kind of leech who couldn't be satisfied. She'd want a bigger part, more lines, more, more, more. And to get it, she'd ruin your career—your life!"

"I can understand what you did to save me." Lolly's voice wobbled and her face was pale. "But, Mom, you can't do this!" She stretched her arms out. "Please, *Matka*?" The Polish word was the plea of a young child waking from a nightmare.

Tears ran down Rikki Popovic's face. She put the knife down.

Buck Foreman came into the room, his pistol aimed. "Please turn around, ma'am," he said, his voice strangely gentle as he brought out a pair of handcuffs.

Michael leaned over Liza, cutting her wrists loose from the duct tape with his pocketknife. "Besides talking to Lolly on the way here, I phoned Buck."

"Thank God I was at Michelle's office in Century City," Buck cut in. "And thank God twice that Michelle was in a meeting."

Yeah—I don't think she'd have been a calming influence, Liza thought.

She looked up at Michael. "And you—you're all right?"

"Just a scratch," he assured her. "Never better."

Then he fainted into her lap.

Liza grabbed hold of him, squawking in pain as he jostled her injured knee. With her ankles still taped to the chair, it was all she could do to keep from toppling over to the floor.

But she stayed upright and held on. Advice from a long-ago first aid course kicked in. *Compress a wound to limit bleeding.*

She wrapped both arms around Michael, clamping both hands over the bloody patch on his shirt.

When the ambulance team arrived, they almost had to pry him away from her.

* * *

Liza only held Michael's hand when he came to in the ER. "If this is heaven," he said, smiling woozily.

"Don't even start, Langley," she told him. "What did you think you were doing?"

"Saving you," he replied. "What did you think you were doing, tied to that chair? It's a freaking cliché."

A doctor pushed through the curtains surrounding the bed. "Back with us, Mr. Langley?" he said. "You're pretty lucky. We stitched up the hole that got stuck in you, and now all you have to do is restore all the blood that leaked out. That requires bed rest"—he gave Liza a reproving look— "and quiet. All right, Mrs. Langley?"

The doctor left, and Michael grinned at her. "Mrs. Langley?"

"They only let family members stay in here," she told him. "You should have seen the fuss Michelle put up. She was annoyed enough already, missing the grand finale of the case."

"Oh. Right." Michael tried to survey his arm in a sling and the bandage on the side of his chest. "What happened to Rikki?"

"Quigley has her," Liza reported. "He's not exactly happy over how that happened, but he's not going to make a fuss."

"He wants the credit," Michael translated. "Not that we'll be grabbing for it. We don't come off looking very smart in this case."

"I'd call it more blinded by loyalty," Liza told him.

"How about Lolly?" he asked.

"Michelle moved in to deal with the media circus. Some idiot on the radio is demanding that she be sent back to Poland—"

"Interesting," Michael commented, "considering she's never been there in her life."

"Alvin Hunzinger is trying to straighten out her immigration status. As for the rest of the fallout, that remains to be seen. Stanley Lumiere hasn't axed her from his film."

"Speaking of films, there's something I need to tell you. I had a script green-lighted. It's not a Stanley Lumiere production—"

"But that's wonderful!" Liza said. "Why didn't you tell me earlier?"

"I was going to, but then that board landed on your leg, and things kept happening." His voice went down a little. "I ruined things between us, acting like an ass until you were ready to divorce me. God, I'm so sorry for that. This time around, I didn't want it to be more of the same, being that insecure guy yelling, 'Ooh! Look what I got!'"

"You're not, and I'm glad you got it," she told him. "So when does production start?"

"Lord knows," he replied. "With my luck, probably tomorrow."

"Well, they said you'll be going home."

Michael smiled. "Maybe I can telecommute."

"You're going to need someone to take care of you. I've volunteered."

He looked at Liza's walker, parked beside her chair. "That's great. And who's going to take care of us?"

"Ysabel," she replied with a smile. "She told Michelle she was already past due for quitting again."

Michael cocked his head, a little confused. "If you're staying, what about your column? What about that dander machine of a dog of yours?"

"Mrs. H. already agreed to take care of Rusty for the duration," Liza assured him. "As for the job—" She smiled. "I can telecommute."

"That only leaves one thing," Michael finally said.

"What's that?"

"I only have one arm working, and I need to scratch. Are you ever going to let go of my hand?"

Liza smiled. "I don't think so."

It was like the first rule of sudoku: "If at first you screw things up, try, try again."

Maybe, together, this time around they could solve the biggest puzzle of all.

Sudo-cues

Out of Symmetry

Written by Oregon's own leading sudoku columnist, Liza K

My husband started out as an agnostic—but I'm afraid now he's become a heretic. He didn't much care if his sudoku puzzles came in symmetrical or non-symmetrical patterns. Lately, however, he's come down pretty heavily on the non-symmetrical side. The symmetrical/non-symmetrical argument has threatened Sudoku Nation with civil war for years. Let's just hope we can keep things civil over the breakfast table.

So where did this whole controversy come from?

The notion of creating arrays of numbers with each number appearing only once in the rows and columns has probably been a mathematical pastime for centuries. The creation of Latin squares, as they were known, was certainly popularized by an eighteenth-century mathematician, Leonhard Euler. These were not puzzles with clues, however—it was more like presenting sudoku solutions. And they also lacked the additional constraint of subgrids where numbers could not recur.

It wasn't until 1979 that a puzzle called "number place" with the restrictions on columns, rows, and subgrids appeared—not in Japan, but in an American puzzle magazine. Although it was uncredited, it is believed to be the work of puzzle constructor Howard Garns.

By the way, it wasn't symmetrical.

These number place puzzles appeared for several years. By the mid-1980s the form was picked up by a Japanese publisher of puzzle magazines, Nikoli. They were called sudoku—short for *"suji wa dokushin ni kagiru."* That's Japanese for "the numbers must be single"—or occur only once. Incidentally, the *"dokushin"* part of the name also means "single" in the sense of "unmarried" or "celibate." So it seems our favorite puzzle with its naked pairs and hidden singles had a double entendre from its early beginnings.

The puzzle people at Nikoli may not have cleaned up the terminology, but they did refine the puzzles, reducing the number of clues and arranging them in symmetrical patterns. It's been suggested that the symmetry notion may have come from crosswords, where the professionally constructed varieties show the same pattern whether the puzzle is viewed right side up or upside down. Although the Japanese love puzzles, their writing system is not crossword-friendly.

It took almost another twenty years before sudoku made its way back into the English-speaking world, mainly thanks to a judge from New Zealand named Wayne Gould. He encountered the puzzle in Tokyo in 1997, became addicted, created a computer program to construct sudoku, and proselytized the puzzle until it was picked up by the *London Times* in 2004. After conquering Britain, sudoku hopped the Atlantic back to America, essentially circumnavigating the globe in about a quarter of a century—and picking up an estimated eighty million fans in some seventy countries along the way.

So what is this whole symmetry thing? It means that sudoku puzzles can repeat the pattern of clues either through mirror reflection or by rotating part of the patterns.

The following seven sudoku blanks show reflective symmetry—if you put a mirror on the dotted line, it would show the same pattern that appears on the other half of the puzzle.

Horizontal and vertical reflections show a mirror image from left to right or from top to bottom.

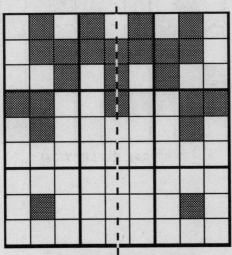

HORIZONTAL REFLECTION

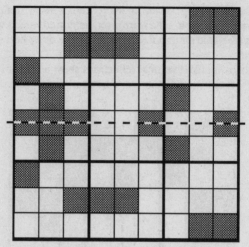

VERTICAL REFLECTION

Diagonal reflection cuts the puzzle in half from upper left to lower right, with the pattern mirrored above and to the right. Anti-diagonal symmetry cuts the puzzle from upper right to lower left, with the pattern recurring in the lower right-hand side.

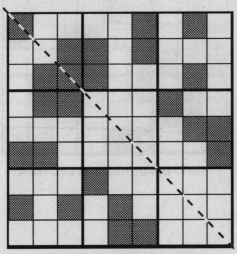

DIAGONAL REFLECTION

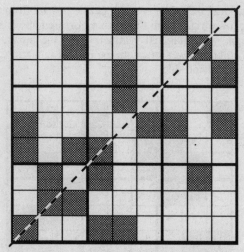

ANTI-DIAGONAL REFLECTION

Symmetry can also combine one axis with another, resulting in puzzles that are simultaneously symmetrical both in the horizontal and vertical directions, or the diagonal and anti-diagonal.

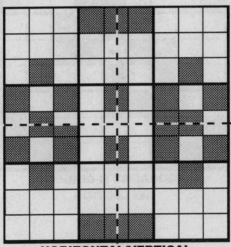

**HORIZONTAL/VERTICAL
REFLECTION**

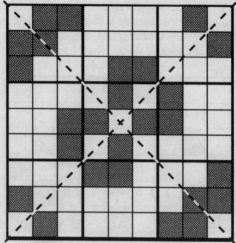

**DIAGONAL/ANTI-DIAGONAL
REFLECTION**

Finally, there's one form that is symmetrical from all viewpoints—side-to-side, top-to-bottom, diagonally, and anti-diagonally. This is called "full dihedral reflection," and I have to admit it's one of my favorites. Sudoku puzzles with this symmetry always remind me of snowflakes (which are, in fact, natural examples of dihedral symmetry).

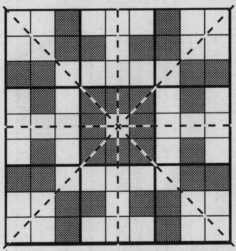

FULL DIHEDRAL REFELECTION

Pretty as reflective symmetry is, you don't see all that many mirror-image puzzles in sudoku. The vast majority, like crosswords, use rotational symmetry to create a pattern of clues. Essentially, this symmetry is created by spinning around or rotating part of an existing image. For instance, if you take half the puzzle and spin it around to the bottom, you end up with 180-degree rotation, as shown below.

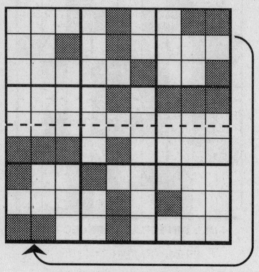

180-DEGREE ROTATION

You can also take a quarter of the puzzle and give it a quarter turn through each remaining quadrant of the puzzle matrix, resulting in a 90-degree rotation. This is another design I particularly like—the results often end up looking like pinwheels.

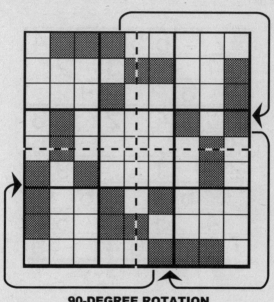

90-DEGREE ROTATION

So now you know all the shapes that go into making symmetrical sudoku. So what's the big difference? They solve the same as non-symmetrical puzzles, don't they?

Well, yes . . . and not exactly.

Let's try to solve this puzzle below, created in 90-degree symmetry.

9			6	5				4
	1				3		2	
		8				9		
	6		4		2			3
8								6
2			1		6		9	
		5				6		
	4		3				8	
7				6	4			9

It's a nice-looking example of its type, although you might well ask, "What's the deal with those hollow numbers?"

Well, they're the dirty little secret of symmetrical sudoku. Those three clues aren't necessary for solving the puzzle. They're only in the grid to complete the design.

Here's the proof—we're going to solve the puzzle without those nonessential clues.

			6	5				4
	1			3		2		
		8				9		
			4		2			3
8								6
2			1				9	
		5				6		
	4		3				8	
7				6	4			9

We'll start with the simplest of the Twelve Steps to Sudoku Mastery: the search for hidden singles. A quick scan through the three subgrids stretching across the center of the puzzle quickly puts us on the track. Moving from left to right, there's a 2 on the first space in row six, which prohibits placing that number in the two open spaces at the bottom of the box at the far right, the only subgrid of the three lacking a 2. Moving right along, a 2 in space six of row four keeps any 2s out of the empty spaces in the top of our target box.

That leaves only two spaces available, and one of those falls into the forbidden zone projected down column eight from the 2 in the second space. Left with only one possible space, we place a 2 in it and move on.

Down in the basement, there's a similar situation going on in the bottom three subgrids. With a 4 in row eight, space two, and another in row nine, space six, four of the possible empty places in the lower right-hand box go right out the window. And the 4 in the top space of column nine puts the proverbial kibosh on one of the two remaining spaces, forcing us to stick a 4 in the final opening.

			6	5				4
	1				3		2	▼
		8				9	▼	▼
			4		2	✗	✗	3
8						2	✗	6
2	❯	❯❯	1	❯❯	❯	✗	9	✗
		5				6	4	✗
	4	❯❯	3	❯❯	❯	✗	8	✗
7				6	4	✗	✗	9

With twenty-five clues and two spaces filled in, that leaves fifty-four spaces to go. And we can find another hidden single from the 4 we just placed. It stretches out a line of forbidden spaces into the box above, putting "do not enter" signs on two of the available spaces. Our old friend at the top of column nine prohibits placing a 4 in another space, while the lucky 4 in space four of row four eliminates two more possible spaces. That forces the placement of a 4 in space seven of row six.

Looking to the left from *that* newly placed 4, we quickly see that it prohibits any repetition of 4s in two spaces in the left-center box. The 4 in row four, space four, eliminates three spaces along the top of the subgrid. And from down in the bottom of column two, the 4 in space eight locks the door on another space right in the middle of the subgrid. There ain't no choice to it—the only place a 4 will fit in those nine spaces is at row five, space three.

Let's continue to track hidden singles in the center tier of subgrids. This center square has six blank spaces, but it takes only two clues to eliminate five of them. Working left from the 6 at the end of row five eliminates three possibilities. And the prohibited zone extending up from the 6 at the bottom of column five scratches three spaces—one of them shared with the previously eliminated set. Five down, and only one space left—the one in the sixth place of the sixth row. What a surprise that it gets a 6.

Working back along row five from the clue at the end of row five helped us to zoom in on one hidden single. Working up from that 6 along column nine eliminates two squares for another possibility in the upper right-hand subgrid. Another 6 in space seven, column seven, does in two more spaces in the square. That leaves two possibilities to place a 6—and the 6 already existing in row one (at space four) denies the possibility in one of them. So the only space that can take a 6 lies three down in column eight, as shown.

That does it for scanning for hidden singles—at least for the time being. The next easiest step would be to search for naked singles—picking a likely space and asking, "Could a 1 go here? A 2?" and so on. Usually, this time-intensive technique is reserved for rows or columns that are almost filled in. We have one like that—column eight, with five known inhabitants. Let's save that time and invest it instead in working out all the possible candidates in the fifty remaining blank spaces. That gives us the above.

And what do you know, if we look carefully along column eight we do indeed find a naked single. Space five represents the only 1 in all of row five. Let's cover up its nakedness with a star and zoom along to space four on column two. There are only two spaces filled in along this column, but if you check, you'll find that space four holds the only 6 in the column. That 6, by the way, along with the one in column six, fills in two of the clues we discarded as nonessential from the original version of the puzzle.

Let's move on.

The next step up in the hierarchy of solving techniques is to check the interactions between boxes and rows or columns. I think this is easier to show in action than to try to describe. If we look along the top tier of subgrids, we see that there's a 3 in the central box (row two, space six) that prohibits any other 3s in that box and all along the second row. In the top-left box, there are five possible places where a 3 could go—three of them in the top row and two of them in row three. Off in the top right-hand box, there are only two possible sites for a 3 to go, both of them in the first row. In this case, row three has two clues already, and the remaining blank space has a 3 in the clue space directly below it, eliminating it as a contender. The interaction of the puzzle mechanics in the box and row means that in the upper right-hand box, a 3 can only appear in the first row—as shown by the starred possibilities. This means that jumping back along the row, we can eliminate the candidates in the first three spaces. A 3 can't possibly go there because it's either in space seven or eight.

So each 3 in each box gets an X through it. And guess what? That leaves only one other candidate in the first space of the puzzle. We can put a star around the 9 in space one and run along the first row and the first column, eliminating a 9 from contention in every space. We also eliminate a 9 in space three in row two, because it's in the same subgrid as the 9 we've just uncovered. (And if you haven't noticed, we've just added the last of the nonessential clues we eliminated at the start of this exercise.)

By the way, we should also clean up after those naked singles we discovered. Sticking the 6 in space two of row four doesn't have too many consequences—the only places to eliminate a 6 as a candidate are the two neighboring spaces in the row. The 1 we found in the fifth space in column eight has more repercussions. It eliminates two possible candidates in the middle-right subgrid along row four at spaces seven and eight. The placement of a 1 in space five of column eight eliminates a candidate at space nine, right down at the bottom of column eight. And zooming up to the top, the elimination of the candidate for 1 in the first space of column eight does away with a candidate up there.

Okay, no shocking discoveries, no new spaces filled, but we've cleared the way for additional developments.

The next step up the Twelve Steps to Sudoku Mastery involves searching for naked pairs. Essentially, that means looking for two spaces that share two and only two candidates. The logic runs like this: If space two on a column has only a 1 and a 9, and space eight on the same column has only a 1 and a 9, then those are the only two places in the column that can hold a 1 or a 9. They can be eliminated as candidates anywhere else along the column.

And what do you know? We've got a naked pair right in the first row—and right next to each other. After all the candidate assassinations in our last move, the only remaining clues in space two and space three along row one are 2 and 7. That means, traveling along the row, we can eliminate 7 as a candidate in spaces six, seven, and eight. It also means that in space eight, there's only one remaining candidate, a 3—but we'll get back to that.

The naked pair still has damage to do in the top-left subgrid. In that box, 2 or 7 will definitely be in the top row, and any other 2 or 7 candidates can be eliminated elsewhere, specifically in row three, space two (adios, 2 and 7), and space three in row two (good-bye, 7—hello, 6 as the only remaining candidate. Let's put a star over it and continue for the time being.)

Meanwhile, back in column eight, what about that 3 we uncovered? Well, placing a 3 at the top of the column eliminates the only other 3 candidate down in the bottom at space nine. And doing that leaves only one viable candidate, the 5. Let's star that and prepare to eliminate some extraneous 5 clues—and some 6 ones as well, from the 6 we uncovered in row two.

Well, cleaning up doesn't exactly start a chain reaction of spaces to be filled—although it does force the placement of a 7 in the last open space in column eight. But things should fall into place in about seven moves. It requires simply finding a hidden single involving a 3, then a naked single and a hidden single, both involving a 5. Then there's a row that has only a single 1, the last 6 to be found, and a hidden single involving a 4. Find all those, and the chain reaction to the end will begin.

Oh, and the reason for my husband's conversion to the non-symmetrical side of sudoku? He tells me he likes to see the vein in my temple swell up when we argue—according to him, it's cute. I guess he feels the same way about that as I do about full dihedral symmetry.

In sudoku as in married life, it's all a question of aesthetics.

Puzzle Solutions

Puzzle from page 26

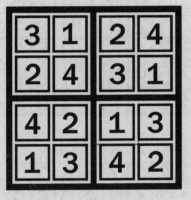

Puzzle from page 36

1	2	3	4	6	8	7	5	9
6	4	7	5	9	3	1	2	8
9	8	5	2	1	7	4	3	6
4	9	8	1	2	5	3	6	7
5	3	6	9	7	4	2	8	1
7	1	2	3	8	6	9	4	5
8	7	4	6	3	9	5	1	2
2	5	9	8	4	1	6	7	3
3	6	1	7	5	2	8	9	4

Puzzle from page 95

9	6	2	7	4	5	3	1	8
8	7	1	3	6	9	5	2	4
5	4	3	8	2	1	7	9	6
4	3	6	1	5	2	8	7	9
7	1	9	4	8	3	2	6	5
2	8	5	9	7	6	1	4	3
6	2	7	5	9	8	4	3	1
3	9	8	2	1	4	6	5	7
1	5	4	6	3	7	9	8	2

Puzzle from pages 133 and 160

5	7	8	6	4	1	9	3	2
6	9	2	3	5	8	4	1	7
3	1	4	7	2	9	6	5	8
8	6	3	2	1	4	5	7	9
9	4	7	8	3	5	2	6	1
2	5	1	9	7	6	3	8	4
7	3	9	1	6	2	8	4	5
1	2	5	4	8	3	7	9	6
4	8	6	5	9	7	1	2	3

Puzzle from page 165

7	3	4	5	8	9	2	1	6
5	1	8	4	6	2	7	3	9
9	2	6	3	7	1	4	5	8
1	4	3	2	9	5	6	8	7
6	9	5	8	4	7	3	2	1
2	8	7	1	3	6	5	9	4
4	5	2	7	1	8	9	6	3
3	6	1	9	5	4	8	7	2
8	7	9	6	2	3	1	4	5

Puzzle Solutions

Puzzle from page 202

9	2	7	6	5	8	1	3	4
5	1	6	9	4	3	8	2	7
4	3	8	7	2	1	9	6	5
1	6	9	4	8	2	5	7	3
8	7	4	5	3	9	2	1	6
2	5	3	1	7	6	4	9	8
3	9	5	8	1	7	6	4	2
6	4	2	3	9	5	7	8	1
7	8	1	2	6	4	3	5	9